WITCH IN TRAINING

A BLAIR WILKES MYSTERY

ELLE ADAMS

1

I'd adopted a monster.

An adorable, fluffy monster, but a monster all the same. Sky the cat sat proudly on my bed, a group of small furred creatures with long tails surrounding him. Mice.

"You're supposed to be a mighty hunter," I told him. "Not build an animal sanctuary. Did you *invite* those mice into the house?"

"Miaow," said the cat, which was the total extent of his vocabulary. Most witches could communicate with their familiar on an instinctive level, but he and I had yet to reach any level of understanding.

"What's up?" Alissa, my flatmate, called to me from the kitchen.

"The cat's bringing mice in again. Alive. And…" I trailed off, seeing a mouse tail under the bed. "Oh no."

"What?" Alissa asked warily. "Did he get into the bubble wrap again?"

"There's none left." My little furred friend had utterly destroyed the re-inflating bubble wrap I'd purchased—partly because I loved the stuff, and partly because I was a walking hazard. Considering my first week in Fairy Falls had been marked by the murder of a client of the paranormal recruitment firm where I now worked, not to mention my being targeted both by said killer and by a vindictive co-worker with a grudge, I'd figured I needed it—and that was without taking my latent clumsiness into account.

No… there was no bubble wrap. Just mice. And underneath the bed was a stack of pieces of cheese. I didn't even want to know how long they'd been there.

"I'm done." I threw up my hands and walked into the kitchen to join Alissa at the breakfast table. "I'm pretty sure he's actually feeding them up so he can eat them later. Has Roald ever done that, or is Sky just weird?"

"He's your cat," she said, taking a bite of toast.

"Thanks." I'd never intended to adopt a cat in the first place. I was only half a witch, but that was apparently enough for me to get adopted by a familiar who I was starting to worry was actually psychotic. "I told you this was a bad idea. He's going to bring half the mice and rats in the neighbourhood right to our home. Is it too late to hand him to an animal shelter?"

"You don't usually have a choice when it comes to familiars."

"Nobody mentioned that." Nobody had told me a lot of things. I'd often felt several steps behind everyone else in my peer group, but learning I was paranormal was on a whole new level. Let alone that I was half fairy, half witch, a fact that had utterly confused most of the people I'd met since my arrival in the paranormal town of Fairy Falls. The divining spells the witches used usually marked me as one or the other. I'd been invited here as a witch, found out I was a fairy, agonised over accidentally deceiving people and then learnt I was both.

I might have only found out I was a paranormal a few

weeks ago, but I knew entirely too little about my own history. Few witches here in Fairy Falls had known my mother. She'd left more than twenty-five years ago, according to Alissa, before the younger generations of witches had been born—and hadn't been seen since. I didn't even know if she was still alive, let alone which of my magical talents I owed to her. I could sense anyone's paranormal type without seeing their face, as well as being able to sense lies. I could also fly, thanks to the wings hidden under my human disguise—or fairy glamour—but I'd only glimpsed them once. I'd barely begun to embrace my witch side, let alone my fairy one.

As for my foster parents, who'd raised me since I was three… they didn't know Fairy Falls existed or that magic was real. I wasn't sure I was looking forward to that conversation, if it ever happened. The paranormal world had strict rules about what you were allowed to tell normals.

Alissa said, "I spoke to my grandmother on the phone. She said you're doing well at learning magical theory, and you might be able to start on the practical stuff soon."

My heart skipped a beat. "Wait, I'm going to get a wand?"

"You need one to cast spells, so—yes."

I did a happy dance. Sky walked into the room halfway through and gave me a look that said *what is that crazy woman doing?* I grinned back. *I'll finally be a proper witch.*

Alissa had become my best friend since I'd come here, and I'd lucked out with her as a flatmate. I knew she'd been singing my praises to her grandmother, who ran the Meadowsweet Coven and pretty much owned the whole town. The least I could do was not mess up my witch training. Let's just say preparatory lessons hadn't exactly been going swimmingly. Hopefully, that would change when I had a wand of my own.

I'd been informed in no uncertain terms that the incanta-

tions from Harry Potter would not work and would probably result in something breaking. I had to admit, I was
afraid that any magic in general might have the same result. I
hadn't grown up in this world, which meant popular culture
was my only prior reference for all things witchy. I'd started
to worry that it was like the difference between learning a
second language from childhood versus learning as an adult.
Magic wouldn't come as easily to me as it would to the
witches who'd been raised here, especially considering the
hundred-and-ten-page long health and safety brochure. I
had the distinct impression they'd added a few dozen pages
especially for me, considering the waves of chaos I'd stirred
up in the few weeks I'd been living here. Not that it was all
my fault, but still.

I didn't give up on a challenge. Not when magic was
everything I'd never known I wanted.

"Madame Grey says you're ready," said Alissa. "She's the
one who has the ability to recommend you. But the person
who gives the final verdict… well. It's Mr Falconer."

I groaned. I should have guessed that Mr Falconer, the
notoriously grumpy wand-maker, was the person who could
ultimately give the verdict on whether I'd be allowed to wield
my own wand or not. "Let's hope he's forgiven me for asking
him probing questions about past clients."

"You were solving a murder at the time. It'll be fine."

"I didn't think he and Mr Bayer even liked one another," I
said.

"He doesn't like anyone."

She wasn't wrong. Mr Falconer didn't scare me as much
as, say, Steve the Gargoyle, the leader of the local police unit,
but he knew what a disaster I'd made of my first week here. I
hoped being half a witch was enough to qualify for a wand.

"The good news is that you can get a broom right away,"
she added. "The High Fliers asked me to invite you to join."

"Er… I think I'll pass."

She grinned. "Thought so. No harm in asking."

"I don't want to have to be fished out of the lake any time soon."

The High Fliers were daredevil Quidditch players, basically. I'd got the hang of my new levitating boots, but broomsticks were a long way off, if ever.

"So when am I going in for wand testing?" I asked. Wands were incredibly expensive but witches usually got one while they were at school, so the coven would cover the costs for me if I passed the tests. Yet another way I could never repay them for helping one seriously confused outsider.

"You have your exam soon, right?"

I nodded, my insides fluttering with nerves. The theory test was fairly basic, but I'd never been much of a fan of exams. "Yep. Rita's going to tell me at my lesson tonight."

"Madame Grey will grade you. If you pass, you'll be able to head right for the wand shop."

"Awesome."

I punched the air. Not long until I was a proper witch.

———

I all but skipped into work that morning, startling Bethan, my co-worker. While it was a relaxed working environment, most of us generally weren't alert before coffee. Especially with three of us currently doing the work of four.

Bethan, who sat at the desk next to mine behind a towering stack of files, sipped from her mug, tucking her straight dark hair behind her ear. "You're in a good mood."

"I'm going to get my own wand. That is, if I pass my theory test," I admitted. "I've been learning the theory for a while, but it's the first time Madame Grey has hinted I might be ready for practical lessons in witchcraft."

"Awesome!" she said. "You'll be able to help repair the coffee machine."

"I doubt that's covered in basic lessons."

Lizzie, our resident tech genius, was responsible for keeping us supplied with coffee, but the technology she created tended to only respond to its owner. Including the possibly-sentient printer in the corner. "Maybe I'll try learning that frog spell."

Lizzie had once made our mutual co-worker, Blythe, temporarily start croaking. While Blythe wasn't here anymore, she'd left us one hell of a mess to clean up.

Lizzie herself, a dark-skinned young woman with braided hair, gave me a grin. "That's a bit advanced for a newbie. Not saying you couldn't pull it off, but there's a fifty-fifty chance of that particular spell rebounding on its owner. It's fickle."

"Might wait a little, then." I still couldn't stop smiling. I liked my new job here at Eldritch & Co, a recruitment firm which matched paranormal employees to clients who needed specialists with the right type of magic. It certainly wasn't dull dealing with wizard businessmen or witches in need of apprentices. But I'd wanted to be able to cast spells of my own ever since I'd found out I was a paranormal myself.

I turned my attention to the client list for the day as Bethan launched into work like a human whirlwind, somehow typing and writing by hand at the same time. Her ability to multitask was down to her family's magic. I hadn't a hope of keeping up, so I concentrated on my own list. And the first name.

Speak of the devil. Mr Falconer, the man who had the power to sell or deny me a wand, was apparently in the market for an assistant again. I was supposed to call him.

Figuring I might as well get our notorious problem client over with first, I dialled his number.

"What?" growled Mr Falconer. My paranormal-sensing ability kicked in, telling me, helpfully, that he was a wizard.

"Hello," I said, with my best customer service voice. "This is Dritch & Co. How may I help you today?"

"I know it's bloody Eldritch & Co. I called you."

So much for being nice. "Yes, this is Blair. Can I help you?"

"I doubt it."

"Then why call me?"

"I'm looking to hire your services. I heard you fancy yourself an investigator. I need a new assistant."

Uh-oh. I'd heard the last one had quit, which explained why he was calling so soon after he'd last hired us a few weeks ago. I hoped my ability to provide someone who could put up with his attitude wouldn't have any bearing on whether he let me have a wand or not.

"A wand-making assistant?" I asked. "What's the criteria?"

"Top level wizards only."

"You mean witches or wizards?"

"Are you deaf? I said, wizards only."

Two strikes against him. "Do you think witches are less competent than wizards, Mr Falconer?" I asked.

"No," he growled. "They're not right for this job."

"Any reason why? Madame Grey and her coven run the whole town. They're the best there is."

"Tradition," he growled.

He could shove that where the sun didn't shine. "I will assemble a list of the best candidates."

Though given his attitude, it was likely that no witch would go within a mile of him. What a miserable old man.

"Do that," he said. "I want grade fives only. Graduates of the Lancashire University of Spellcraft. Highly ranked in every specialist area of wizardry. No other commitments or relationships with any coven other than their own."

"Is that all?" I asked, sarcasm dripping from my voice. "Want me to call the ones who can recite the Lord's Prayer while bungee jumping as well?"

There was a dial tone as he hung up. Oops. I scowled at the phone.

"I wouldn't mess with him," Bethan said.

"I can't help it. He's just asking for trouble. Did you know he refuses to work with women at all?"

"Oh, he's known for that," Bethan said, not batting an eyelid. "That'd be because the Meadowsweet Coven charged him over an infraction. He's still bitter about it."

"But they still buy their wands from him?"

"Yes. Since he refuses to train anyone else to make wands and nobody does it better, we don't have any choice but to keep buying them from him until someone else comes along. We're secretly hoping he'll train up an assistant who will take over, but nobody can stand to be around him long. I think the last candidate moved to France."

"Great." I wished there was something I could do to help. But I didn't want to subject any of my fellow witches to his attitude. "Right, I'll get the list together. He's not asking for much, is he? And that's assuming these highly ranking wizards can put up with him. Didn't he only hire us a few weeks ago?"

"Yeah, they never last long," commented Bethan. "You might have to sift through previous candidates first."

She wasn't wrong. Half the first list of candidates had already either turned down interviews, failed to secure the position, or angered the man so much that he kicked them out. There was also a witch who'd tried to sneak in by disguising herself as a man, but no magic could fool the wand-maker's eyes.

What a piece of work.

I made call after call, heard excuse after excuse, and eventually, called the man himself again.

"Where's my candidate?" he growled.

"We're working on it," I said. "Is there a major wizard family in this town you *haven't* started a feud with?"

"Yes. Mr Franklyn."

"He said you should do something unmentionable."

"Are you trying to be difficult, Miss Wilkes?"

"Nope." *Not me, anyway.*

"Then try harder."

He hung up. Bethan gave me a pitying look. "I can hand you over some of my candidates if it helps. Pretty sure I have a fifth level wizard here somewhere."

"Wait, are you sure?"

She nodded. "It'll get him off your back. I imagine wand-making pays well, if you can ignore the guy's personality."

I'd have considerable difficulty holding my tongue if I'd been in their position, but it wasn't up to me to decide. "I'll call him."

I took the paper from her, and dialled the number of Bethan's most promising candidate.

"Are you interested in learning the art of wand-making?" I rattled off my speech, making it sound as appealing as possible, and finishing by mumbling Mr Falconer's name.

"Sure," said the candidate. "That does sound like what I'm looking for."

"Wait, you want to?"

"Yes, I do."

"Then I'll give you his number."

Success! Now he had no excuses. I was one step closer to a wand of my own.

———

On the way back from work, I took a detour via the high street to meet Alissa, who worked at the local hospital. It was easy to spot the wand-maker's shop on the corner—a gloomy place that looked like the sun had never shone on its brick facade. Wands were lined up in the window, but not in a particularly artful way. All of them looked the same—like sticks filed down to the same shape. I'd seen witches and wizards decorate theirs with accessories, but they must buy them somewhere else. One wand lay separate from the others, in its own case. Unlike the others, it was bright silver and decorated with ribbons that surely hadn't been applied by the wand-maker himself. I peered closer—

"You!" said Mr Falconer, slamming open the door. "What are you doing?"

I blinked innocently. "Walking home. I just stopped to look, since I'm getting my own wand this weekend."

He moved closer to me. A tall thin man with stringy grey hair and a face that looked like he'd never smiled in his life, he had the manner of a dragon defending its hoard when he moved in front of the wand display, as though expecting me to try to steal one. "I'll be the judge of that."

Behind him, a mouse streaked out of the slightly open door. I jumped sideways, and he cursed, lunging forwards. Picking up the mouse by the tail, he carried it back into the shop.

I followed, my curiosity officially piqued, as he dropped the mouse into a cage on the front desk. Several other rodents crouched inside.

"What are you doing in here?" he snapped at me.

"You picked up a small woodland creature," I pointed out. "You can't blame me for being a little curious."

"Curiosity killed the—" He broke off with a glance at the mice, which squeaked frantically, pawing at the cage bars. It was plain to see that they were pretty distressed.

"Why are you keeping so many mice in here?" He hadn't struck me as the type to have pets. "I think you'd get along with my cat."

He narrowed his eyes at me. "Get. Out."

Message received. Making a mental note to ask Alissa who was the best person to report animal cruelty to, I walked out of the wand-maker's shop.

The door slammed behind me.

2

"He did what?" asked Alissa. "He has mice in his shop? Are you joking?"

Frantic squeaking followed from the top drawer in my room. Our attempt to evacuate my unwanted visitors was *not* going well.

"Apparently," I said. "Is there an epidemic? I've had enough of rodents in my underwear drawer. At this rate I'll come back from my spell lesson to find a whole rodent metropolis. Can't they live somewhere other than in our flat?"

"Roald would kill them if they moved to another part of the house, like a normal feline," she said.

"Nothing about Sky is normal." I gave the cat an accusing look, where he sat licking a paw on my bed. "They're just going to have to stay here while I'm at my magic lesson. I'm already running late."

I'd started taking night classes on magical history and theory, while I waited to be approved for my practical assessments. I hoped I'd retained enough information to pass next week's theory exam. I'd never been particularly studious, and it'd been a while since I'd graduated from university. My history degree had not done much to prepare me for being a witch.

"Good luck!" Alissa waved me off, and I grabbed my shoulder bag before leaving for the witches' meeting place.

The witches' headquarters was a large brick building that belonged to Madame Grey, and served as a meeting place, adult education centre and convention hall all rolled into one. Rita, my tutor, held my lessons there—for now, one-to-one, at least until I caught up to at least some of the other witches and wizards. She was eccentric, to say the least, and her teaching methods ranged from interesting lectures to deciding I needed to stand outside in a storm to see if I turned out to be a weather-witch. Every witch had one primary talent. I'd been tested for every type of magic possible, and it looked like the only major gift I was going to have was my ability to sense paranormal types and tell if someone was lying. Both were very useful skills, so I wasn't complaining.

Several other witches and wizards milled around in the entrance hall. While Rita had volunteered herself as my mentor, there were other classes here at the same time, mostly for wizards and witches who'd missed out on part of their education for some reason or other. Or those who were over-enthusiastic learners looking to earn some extra credits towards their degree courses. First in line was Helen Banks, a blond woman who beamed when she spotted me. "Hey, Blair!"

"Hey," I said, slightly less enthusiastically. A twenty-something schoolteacher at the local academy, she'd taken it upon herself to get me more involved in the community, by any means necessary. Every time I ran into her, I spent twenty minutes trying to extricate myself from things she'd volunteered me for.

"You're here for your lesson, right?" She gave me another sunny smile.

"Yep. I'm looking for—"

"You have to speak to me afterwards!" she said. "I heard you're getting your own wand, and we're looking for volunteers at the academy dance show—"

"Er, that's great, but I'm busy that day." I spotted Rita and made my way over to her with relief. Thankfully, nobody else occupied the classroom she'd picked out for our lessons. To say my attempts to learn basic potion-making weren't going spectacularly was an understatement. Despite my best efforts, the table in the corner, along with the floor underneath and the walls behind it, were splattered with the remnants of accidental explosions.

"Helen got you again?" Rita asked.

"She tried," I admitted. "What's she here for this time?"

"Advanced potion making. She told me to give you these." She indicated a mile-high stack of books on the desk.

"Advanced? I've barely read the basics."

"She likes to mentor the newbies. Humour her. Anyway, have you been practising wand movements?"

"Yes." I looked like a complete tit waving my hand around without any magical effects to back it up, but considering how easy it was to accidentally make the wrong movement and cast another spell entirely, I needed all the practise I could get. Even the most basic spells involved remembering a string of complicated patterns, which I'd practised until my wrist ached. The more complex spells tended to involve props, ingredients, rituals—all the extra parts of being a witch—not to mention working alongside someone else. The other witches didn't all know I was half fairy and most didn't seem to care about that type of thing, but I couldn't help feeling a little concerned for my future classmates. Assuming I passed my first exam.

"So," she said. "Your own wand. Are you excited?"

"Yes," I said. "Absolutely."

"It'll come with the safety settings on to begin with," she said. "Standard procedure."

"For five-year-olds." That was the age most witches and wizards began training. I was a little behind to say the least, but it was okay. I'd catch up, and there was no reason I wouldn't be turning people into frogs with the best of them by the end of the year. "That doesn't sound like something Mr Falconer would come up with."

"No, the schools' health and safety department did. *So* many accidents. People being turned into animals… even the occasional flying car."

"You've read Harry Potter." Rita leapt a dozen points in my esteem. She was a little hands-on with her lessons sometimes, but she was far less scary than Madame Grey.

"Of course I have," she said. "It's not entirely inaccurate on some things, as far as the witch academy goes, but the coven dropped the mandatory pointed hats because they have a tendency to get stuck in doorways."

I grinned. "I bet they do."

"I miss the capes, though," she admitted. "It was easier to tell a witch's coven by sight, though it naturally made things harder for outsiders." A pause. "Not that I'm implying you're an outsider."

"I am—or I was. But I don't mind, honestly."

"Some of the younger witches really want to fit in."

"I gave up on that a while ago," I said. But while I'd never thought of myself as magical, I fit in here like I'd never fit anywhere else.

"You'll feel more at home when you have a wand," she said. "If you take to it immediately, I'll put you on an accelerated programme so you'll catch up to the junior witches in no time."

Meaning: if I spent the next year working my tail off, I might have the skill of an eleven-year-old. No complaints here.

"You've done so much for me," I said. "I couldn't ask for anything else."

"You've missed out on a lot," she said. "But you're coping well."

They were all so nice to me. Even Madame Grey, whose brand of niceness was more of the stern schoolteacher type, but I wouldn't expect any less from the leader of the coven who ruled the whole town. And she was Alissa's grandmother, which was a plus.

"When's my exam, then?" I asked.

"I can pencil you in to take the theory test on Friday evening?"

"Sounds good," I said.

"Then you'll be able to apply for a wand that very weekend. Mr Falconer will be informed."

"Mr Falconer seemed to think I can help him find a new assistant," I said. "He called my workplace and talked me into helping him."

She frowned. "And has he said why he keeps losing his assistants?"

"No. I thought it was a given: they all hate him."

"There's something not quite right about that man," she muttered.

"Don't you buy your wands from him? Aren't they the best in town?"

Rita's own wand flipped into her hand. Like her arms, it was decorated with a series of bright-coloured bands. "The *only* ones in town."

"I heard. So you think I can do it?"

She smiled. "Personally? I think you absolutely can. Madame Grey does, too. Anyway, let's run through the exercises again."

I rose to my feet, brimming with a newfound confidence at their faith in me. No witch could borrow another's wand and use it without it backfiring, so I'd been reduced to dancing around waving a stick in the air and generally feeling like a complete prat when I did the exercises.

"You're slightly off-centre," she commented, observing my right hand's movements. "Left—not that far, otherwise you'll cast a shrinking spell."

"It seems a bit risky," I commented. "What if you get the angle slightly wrong and end up casting the wrong spell? Surely that happens a lot."

"The safety settings should prevent the worst mishaps, but yes, it happens."

I made a mental note to learn as many counter-spells as possible beforehand. I was as uncoordinated as a basket of baby kittens learning to walk on a good day. I'd once gone to a ballet lesson and managed to kick my neighbour in the eye, so I'd sworn off any similar hobbies, but I wanted a wand badly enough to risk the indignity.

"Focus," she said, as I faltered on the movement of a levitation spell.

More like flail. Wand-waving was a serious upper-arm workout. I demonstrated locking and unlocking spells, levitation and conjuring. There were whole volumes of spells I wouldn't get to for years, but the curriculum had been designed to prioritise the spells young witches and wizards were likely to need on a daily basis.

"Good," she said, clapping her hands in a jangling noise. "I think that's as much as I can teach you. Unless you'd like to join the Young Advanced Witches Club?"

"How old is its average member?"

"Eight."

"I think I'll give it a miss. It's bad enough that Helen keeps trying to get me to help out at the academy's dance festival. If I wanted to make a fool of myself in front of a bunch of schoolchildren, I'd have signed up to join in regular witch classes before I learnt the basics."

"Some of the witches do think you'd do better in a class-room environment," she said. "We'll re-evaluate once you have your own wand. Now, show me that levitation spell again."

———

The following morning brought an unwelcome surprise: the candidate who'd signed up to be interviewed by Mr Falconer had called my office last night, leaving a message to say that he was no longer interested in the position.

"Great," I said. "Back to square one."

"He said no?" asked Bethan.

"Last night, after hours. Changed his mind pretty quick-ly," I said.

"Everyone knows what Mr Falconer's like. I'm surprised he got that far."

I frowned. "Yeah, but why back out now? He wanted the job. I guess he didn't know I'd take the fall if he turned it down, but come on."

"Falconer?" Lizzie asked, pausing beside my desk on her way to the printer. "The last candidate did that, too. But I was sure he'd found a good one this time."

"Yeah, weren't you dealing with him a few weeks ago?" I asked.

She nodded. "I found him someone. I guess he didn't like the working environment. Not the first time."

"No, I gathered. *How* many times has he hired this company in the last year?"

"I lost count at twenty." She glanced down at the candidate list. "Three of those are already no-shows."

"Twenty?" I echoed. "And you found him someone every time?"

"And every time, the candidate left."

"Did they all leave town, or the country?" I asked.

Lizzie shrugged. "I don't know. We have a lot of clients."

"Do many of them go through twenty assistants in a year?" I asked.

"No," said Bethan, "but most employers have some redeeming qualities. It *is* weird, though, but what choice do we have? He pays us well. And he's the only wand-maker in town."

I blinked. "Guys. I realise this is a magical town and not exactly like anything I'm used to, but I'd start to get a little concerned if someone got through twenty assistants in a year and they all vanished off the face of the earth."

Lizzie tapped her fingers on the desk. "You're right. Bethan…?"

Bethan's brows shot up.

"I wouldn't ask it of you," I said, "but you can do it in two minutes while I'm on the phone and still end up with four times as much work done as me."

Bethan couldn't deny Lizzie had a point, and neither could I. I would have envied her epic multitasking skills if I was the competitive sort, but I wasn't. It was impossible to compete with someone who had magical advantages.

"Oh, all right," said Bethan. "I'll look into the other candidates. But you do need to find him someone today, Blair. If not, he'll come and gripe at Veronica, which will cause *her* to gripe at us, and I already have to deal with finding a professional unicorn-handler. Let me tell you, that's almost as bad as the wand-maker."

"Unicorn-handler?" I said. "Want to swap?"

"Nice try, but nope." She grinned. "I *will* get those candidate details sorted for you, no problem."

She began to tap on her computer keyboard, while Lizzie shot me a sympathetic look and returned to her own desk. Leaving me with the wand-maker's increasingly bizarre situation.

The candidates weren't just declining because the old man was as appealing an employer as Professor Snape. Something else was going on.

While Bethan got the details, I could do worse than call up the candidate and find out why he'd made his abrupt decision.

He picked up after a few moments.

"Hello?" I said. "This is Dritch & Co. We found you a job yesterday. Why did you decline? You seemed keen on the job yesterday."

He hesitated. "I called the last assistant and couldn't get through. I heard he left the country."

"That's what I heard, too. Why?"

"Then I called the one before. He disappeared, too."

"That's… unfortunate."

He exhaled. "There's something weird going on. They all —all—mysteriously disappeared, won't answer their phones, and have all but disappeared from existence. Everyone who's taken on that job in the last year."

I frowned. "That's just—weird. Why would he be so desperate to hire someone only to get rid of them? Unless he's planning human sacrifices, or…" I should probably not be saying this to the candidate who until yesterday, might have actually wanted the job. "Well, my co-workers and I are looking into the situation, but he needs to find someone today…"

"Not me," he said firmly. "This is too weird. I don't want to die."

"You're not going to die." But how could I be sure? If asked to pick out which of the residents of Fairy Falls I'd met so far might be a potential murderer, Mr Falconer would rank top of the list, but being an antisocial grump wasn't a crime.

The guy clearly wasn't going to change his mind, so I ended the call and turned back to my desk. What now? Mr Falconer wouldn't take no for an answer. But what *was* he doing to his assistants? Surely not murdering them. After all, he knew I'd caught one killer.

Fishy. Definitely fishy.

I took an extra dose of motivational coffee before I called the man himself.

"What do you mean, the candidate declined?" he yelled into the phone.

"Everyone declined," I said brightly. "Funny, that."

"I don't find anything funny about it."

I doubted he'd ever found anything funny in his life.

"He seems to think something odd keeps happening to your candidates," I said to him. "He's not willing to take the risk."

"What did you tell him?"

I had the presence of mind to yank the phone away so his yelling didn't burst my eardrum. Both Bethan and Lizzie winced in sympathy.

"I didn't tell him a thing. I'm just passing on the message. He said every one of your previous assistants has vanished without trace. Looking at the information available, that appears to be true."

"Don't talk to me like I'm a fool," he snapped.

"Look, Mr Falconer. It's obvious to me that there's something odd going on. Legal or not, I can't say for sure. But people are talking. You can't hide this forever, and frankly, I'm surprised you thought you could keep it a secret from me, considering you've hired Dritch & Co to help you twenty times in a year. Surely you guessed someone would notice."

"Your colleagues aren't as impertinent as you are."

That was friendly. "Why not just tell me? I'm hardly going to report you to Steve the Gargoyle for scaring off your staff, but the fact that you keep hiring my company is a cause for suspicion."

"There are no other recruitment firms in town, and you have a better chance of convincing potential candidates to apply."

Given his manners, he might well be right. But how had nobody noticed before?

"Come and speak to me in person," he insisted. "The information is too delicate to share over the phone."

"I can hardly walk out of work now, Mr Falconer."

"Ask your boss. Or drop by later, it's all the same to me. But I *will* get that candidate." And he hung up.

Wow. Someone really needed a hobby.

I took in a couple of steadying breaths, looking at the silent phone. One call had completely wiped out the effects of the coffee. "Do you think the boss will let me head over there and see him?"

Bethan looked at me like I'd announced I had a week to live. "He asked you to go to him in person?"

"Yep. I think the people in the building next door heard, too." I rubbed my ear. "He didn't deny there's something odd going on."

"No, well." She held up a stack of papers. "I got this printed off, and I'd say you're right to be suspicious. Check out these records."

I took the papers and skimmed through the names of the previous applicants.

"Every one of them has inactive social media accounts," she went on. "The last time any of them went online varies, but it looks like they all lasted a few weeks at the job, so he doesn't murder them right away."

"You really think he kills them?"

"No," she said. "I think he probably does something traumatic. None of us actually knows what kind of magic goes into wand-making. Maybe it erases their memories or causes them to lose their minds, or…"

"We're complicit," said Lizzie. She wasn't smiling. "If I'd known when I was dealing with him before, I'd have told the candidate not to apply."

"But… okay, I'm not blaming you guys," I said. "I'm just confused as to why nobody else in town has noticed."

"You've worked here long enough to see the other clients we get, haven't you?" said Bethan. "They have all sorts of weird requests. I dealt with five last week who wanted temporary interns or people to help with a one-off job. It's not so unusual. Neither is danger. Hence the number of safety forms I'm dealing with for this unicorn-handler." She waved a hand at the teetering pile of papers on her desk. "We work with weirdos. It takes a special kind of weird to catch our attention."

I nodded. "Yeah, I'm a normal, so weirder-than-weird catches my attention pretty fast. Do you think I should go and see him? He knows I'm living with Madame Grey's granddaughter, and even he respects her."

"Can't hurt," she said. "I mean, it can, but take your phone and some other precautions. Also, get a note from the boss."

"You seem keen to send me into danger," I quipped.

"I honestly want to know what he did with his assistants," she said. "I don't think he killed them. Unless there's some secret ritual known only to wand-makers that keeps backfiring… in which case, you'll be fine, since you aren't applying to work for him."

"I'll find out." I got to my feet. "But first, the boss."

3

Veronica looked at me across her desk, which was a large grey model this morning. Her office decorations varied depending on her mood. Today, the theme was steel grey fittings and large computer monitors, like some kind of high-tech futuristic workshop.

"What is it, Blair?" she asked. She wore a smart suit and had the same fine hair as her daughter, except silver-white instead of dark brown. Tall and willowy, she had a commanding presence despite her eccentric taste in décor.

"I'm helping a candidate find an assistant, and he's asked me to come and speak to him in person," I explained. "Mr Falconer, the wand-maker. It's come to my attention that something might be happening to his assistants, and he refused to tell me any more information over the phone."

"Wand-maker?" she asked. "Oh, he's a recurring client. Terrible manners."

"I know," I said. "So—can I go and speak to him now? He's refusing to budge and insists I'm to find him an assistant one way or another. I think it's the best way to get him to cooperate."

"Hmm. He's never asked us to visit the place before. Aren't you applying for a wand of your own?"

"After I take the first theory test," I said.

"Excellent. Then you'll be able to take on some of our trickier clients."

Hmm. I dreaded to think who might be trickier to deal with than Mr Falconer. Maybe unicorns.

"Thank you," I said to her. "I'll be back as soon as I can."

I'd rather deal with problem clients over the phone, but with Mr Falconer's threat hanging over my head, I needed to get him off my back. And get answers.

I walked quickly down the road, turning into the high street where the wand-maker's place stood at the corner. Again, it looked closed and neglected. He needed to replace a pane of glass in the window, and the door had seen better days.

I knocked this time, and the door opened sharply. Mr Falconer stood waiting, wearing his usual sour expression. "Blair Wilkes," he said.

"That's me." I ducked into the shop. I wore my leather levitating boots—they passed as work-appropriate and the boss never looked too closely—and smart casual clothing, but he looked at me as though I'd trampled mud into the carpet. A nervous flutter in my stomach reminded me I was alone with someone who might possibly be murdering his assistants.

Relax. The boss knows you're here. If nothing else, maybe I could grab one of the wands if anything weird happened. Though I'd heard they only worked for their owners, nobody else. Still, one of them was destined to be mine. If I got through the cantankerous man in front of me.

"So, what is it you couldn't tell me over the phone?" I asked.

"The job," he said through gritted teeth, "is cursed."

I blinked. "I'm sorry, what? It's cursed how?"

"Every candidate I hire falls victim to the same curse," he said. "Within two weeks of being hired. All of them."

"You might want to be a bit more specific. What is this curse, exactly?"

His gaze shifted. I became aware of a faint squeaking noise coming from the desk. The cage of mice remained where it'd been before. I looked at the mice. Then I looked back at him.

"You've got to be joking." Laughter bubbled up in my throat and I fought to keep it reined in. "Someone's been turning all your assistants into mice?"

"For a year," he said, with an expression that suggested I'd be joining them if I dared laugh at him.

"And you didn't tell anyone?"

He gave me an ugly look. "I'm the best spellcaster in the entire town, Miss Wilkes. If I can't undo the spell, nobody else can."

The urge to laugh disappeared. He was one scary man. "Er, aren't the witches skilled at this type of thing, too?"

"It's not a spell," he snapped. "I've read every book on the subject in existence. I made my career on spells. This is a curse. Unlike regular spells or even those handmade ones, curses don't require a wand. Anything could have set it off."

"Set it off?" I echoed. "Didn't a person do it?"

"Evidently," he growled. "But I fail to see who might have anything to gain from pranking my assistants. If they wanted to sabotage me, they would have targeted me directly. So they're a coward, and when I catch them, I'll make them live to regret ever setting foot in this town."

Sparks flew from the wands displayed in the window, ricocheting off the walls. I ducked, my arms over my head, until they stopped. *Whoa.*

"All right," I said, my heart thumping with panic. "So you

want me to help? Because I know even less about curses than I do about spells."

"If you *can* help, which I sincerely doubt."

I took in a deep breath. "Tell Madame Grey—"

"Absolutely not."

"But she's the most knowledgeable witch there is. If the job is cursed, then sooner or later you'll run out of people to hire. Wouldn't it be easier if you got to the root of the problem?"

His jaw clenched. "The problem is that I have no bloody clue who did it."

"Then I'm not sure I can help. I wasn't even here a year ago."

He stepped in close. "Isn't that a pity? You poked your nose into my life, and now you're going to have to prove your worth. Aren't you scheduled to pick up a wand soon?"

"Yes," I said warily.

"Then if you don't help me get to the bottom of this thorny little problem, you will never own a wand of your own."

"That's not necessary," I said. "I'm not an expert. I'm pretty sure my cat knows more about spells than I do."

"I hired you. You're to do your job." Spit flew from his mouth.

I took a step back out of range. "I'm not a detective. Mr Bayer—that was a case of being in the wrong place at the wrong time. I wouldn't know where to begin with whoever cursed your job."

"Isn't that a pity? If you're going to put off my potential candidates and make me look like a fool, then you deserve to deal with the consequences yourself."

"I'm not putting anyone off. I think hearing a job is cursed is enough to deter most applicants, to be honest. Most people don't have any ambitions to turn into rodents."

"Do you think you're amusing, Miss Wilkes?"

"Some people do." Okay, even my cat didn't, but that was beside the point. "Look, I'll try to help, but I can't make any promises. If nobody else in town has answers, I doubt I have the magical solution. But I can try."

Madame Grey would counter his empty threats with real ones, but there were twenty people stuck as mice, trapped in here with him. I doubted he was an attentive pet owner. Also, I couldn't help wondering who'd have the audacity to put a curse on one of the scariest people in town.

"For a start, when did this start happening?" I asked. "A year or more ago, the client said. Was there a particular issue with your last client at the time?"

"No," he snarled.

That was helpful. I could tell he was going to be perfectly pleasant and cooperative to work with.

"I have to start somewhere," I said. "Who was the first assistant to be affected? Wait—what are you telling these people's families? Don't they come here asking questions?"

"Each has an effective cover story," he said. "They left town, they left the country… plenty of people do."

"So the loved ones of twenty people think they'll never see them again."

Unbelievable. It wasn't fair on the victims at all. As much as I wanted to leave Mr Falconer to stew in his own misery and grumpiness, I couldn't leave the mice there. I approached the cage, looking inside. "There are only four mice. Where are the others?"

"They escaped."

I groaned. "You mean to say the victims aren't even here? They might have been eaten by cats, or…" Wait. The mice in my flat.

But Sky hadn't eaten them… had he known they were human?

Mr Falconer loomed over me. "I want you to find me answers, Blair. Now go, before I change my mind about ensuring your silence."

I had no doubt he could do some serious damage with his wand collection. I'd met one person with the ability to mess with memories and had no intention of repeating the incident. Though my inner lie detector hadn't gone off, it was plain to see Mr Falconer wasn't telling me everything. I'd have to work on getting through to him later. For now, I'd look at the information I had, and learn who the candidates were before their untimely rodent fates. I could sense what type of paranormal someone was, but that didn't extend to finding the source of a curse. I hadn't even been able to tell the mice were once human, which seemed a gaping loophole in my skills. Maybe it only worked on humans, or people who looked like them. Not animals. Even if those animals were once wizards themselves.

Magic was much more complicated than I'd thought. And to think I'd been confident I could pick up a wand and make it work for me. How to do that when my fate rested in the hands of a man who'd somehow managed to curse his assistant's job?

"One last thing," he added. "Don't you dare tell the other witches."

"Seriously? I'm not allowed to ask for help?"

"It's my business, and if you tell them, you'll *definitely* never be one of them."

Right. Part of me wondered if he'd set the curse off himself in a temper against his former apprentices, but if he wanted to curse someone, he had a whole arsenal of weaponry and the creativity to use it. More likely, he'd angered the wrong person and the curse had hit his apprentice instead.

"I'll solve this," I said, eying the squeaking mice. Never

mind my wand—twenty innocent people were now counting on me to help them.

———

"He said, 'don't tell the witches'?" asked Alissa.

I sat across from her on the sofa. "Yes, I know I'm telling *you*, but I'm trusting you not to tell him. My co-workers are suspicious, but if I tell them, they'll tell Veronica, and word will make it back to him."

She blinked at me, absently stroking Roald. "Don't worry. We're not all gossips, not when the secret is important. But he can't deny you a wand."

"We'll get to that part later," I said. "It sounds like he's angered dozens of people. One of them must have cursed the job. It seems weird that they'd target his assistant and not him, but maybe they had good reasons."

"Was he angry? I don't think you should go back there alone."

"More like humiliated," I said. "This person's running circles around the town's best spellcaster and he can't do a thing. Which I suppose is what they meant to do. The problem is, everyone hates him."

She pursed her lips. "Given the nature of the curse, it's safe to say the caster was a witch or wizard. Or had the help of one of them."

"Aren't all his clients witches or wizards, though?" I said. "I got the files of the past employees who vanished. There are no common factors between them, only that they all worked for him for a couple of weeks before the curse came on. He refused to tell me any more than that, so I'm going by guesswork."

"Hmm," she said. "Normally I'd say put a spell on him to

make him more talkative, but he's bound to see through that. So maybe… talk to some of the people he's worked with."

I nodded. "I think he's only ever had one assistant at a time. It's a bit confusing. He also hasn't hired Dritch & Co before last year, so I guess he must have found his previous assistants in person rather than hiring a company to do it. And the new applicants don't know what exactly happened to the previous assistants. I don't *think* they'd intentionally let it slip, but he's seriously intent on not letting Madame Grey find out."

"She will," said Alissa. "But not if it gets you into trouble. Also, you're probably right… maybe ask among the witches? I'm sure someone will have had an argument with him."

"It was a year ago that the curse came on," I said. "Which is why I'm not the best person for the job, because I wasn't even here. I don't know the relationships and disagreements that have taken place over the last year. Let alone before."

"But you *do* have the ability to sense lies."

"There is that," I said. "All right. I'll ask Rita, maybe… oh, yeah. Make sure Roald doesn't get near those mice. I think— they're the former assistants. Some of them."

"What?" Her eyes widened. "*Oh.* Sky must have worked out they're human. Smart cat."

"Yep," I said. "Too smart. And I think we need to get those mice somewhere else in case another predator catches them. Those poor assistants' families think they're either dead or permanently out of contact."

She wrinkled her nose. "Ugh. I can't believe he left them hanging because he was too embarrassed to admit someone cursed him."

"Tell me about it," I said. "All right. I'm off to my lesson."

4

My magic lesson was a disaster. I dropped the stick I was using as a practise wand so many times that Rita threw up her hands in despair. "What's bothering you?"

"Wands," I said stupidly. "What if I'm not witch enough to have one?"

"Don't be ridiculous," she said. "Not every witch has both parents as witches or wizards. It's more common here, because we're so close-knit, but it's not unheard of for witches or wizards to marry normals."

Or even non-humans. Like fairies. There was still so much I didn't know about my own history… and now I might never get the chance to pursue my own magical talents, thanks to Mr Falconer's ridiculous request.

"Okay," I said. "The wand-maker seemed pretty insistent that he only sells to witches and wizards, nobody else."

"Oh, him," she said. "Don't worry, he won't discount you as a half witch. We don't see things that way. If you're magical at all, you're one of us. Even he can't deny it."

"Okay. He's kind of… irritable. Is there anyone he's

particularly ticked off recently?" Probably too vague a question, but I had to start somewhere.

"Recently?" she echoed. "He hasn't left that blasted shop of his in years. Practically a recluse. He's worse than Mr Bayer was. At least Bayer was working on useful inventions for the common good. All Mr Falconer's wands are practically identical and he hasn't changed the recipe in years. He's just avoiding people. He's a miserable man."

"I gathered," I said. "So he's never been married?"

She burst out laughing. "No. Certainly not. To my memory, he's always been the same grumpy recluse for as long as anyone has lived here. If he's ever been involved with anyone, I'm not aware of it."

I thought not. An angry ex-partner or spouse might unleash that type of curse, if they didn't care about the consequences for the people who ended up as mice. But I doubted anyone could have put up with his attitude for an extended period of time. Even if he'd been a catch when he'd been younger, his personality was repellent. Besides, the curse had only kicked in in the last year.

"No other relatives?" I asked.

"Not to my knowledge," she said. "I'm the wrong person to ask about family trees, but as far as I know, he's the last of his bloodline."

Hmm. If I wanted to delve into the past, the person to ask was Vincent, the oldest vampire in town. He'd been polite to me, but slightly scary, and my talking to him had ticked off the werewolves. While the wolf pack had somewhat forgiven me for accidentally getting their chief's beloved daughter temporarily stuck in her wolf form, not to mention accidentally sending a former sort-of-rogue to their pack, I'd been keeping out of their way lately.

On the other hand, there was no need to go digging too far into history. Since the town had so few newcomers, most people would have been around a year ago. Unfortunately, since I was the only recent newbie, that still covered the town's entire population of witches and wizards. Or at least those who were capable of casting curses.

"Do you need a wand for every magic type?" I asked. "I mean, there are types that require different props, right?"

"Technically, you don't," she said. "But wand magic is the most basic. Other, more advanced magic, is taught at a much later age."

At this rate, I might catch up by the time I was forty. I barely had a handle on the different definitions—hex, curse, and spell. Unlike hexes, curses didn't need to be cast directly at the target and could even be used from a distance, but I needed to ask the right questions to find out how one would go about messing with a job, as opposed to a person. My only experience of hexes so far had been what Blythe had done to Callie, turning her into a wolf, while I had no experience of curses at all.

"So I won't be hexing Blythe anytime soon?" I asked.

"Hexes are more likely to rebound on the caster at first," she said.

"And curses?" I asked casually. "Do people frequently curse their enemies here? The guy who runs the apothecary said so once."

"Curses generally require more props. They're very advanced magic, tricky to work—and impossible to break without knowing the caster. You'd have to really hate someone to put a curse on them."

Yeah, I figured. The person who'd cursed Mr Falconer plainly hadn't been bothered that twenty innocent people had also been caught in the spell, which seemed callous to say the least. Most witches were responsible with the way they used magic.

"The worst ones are illegal, right?" I asked. I still hadn't memorised the extensive paranormal rulebook, but luckily, most of the laws required actual skill at magic to break. I was in no danger of accidentally cursing someone.

"Yes. There are a hundred and twelve illegal types of curses, but I think only Madame Grey knows them all."

"Is there a list of the illegal curses?"

She gave a slight smile. "Not getting any ideas about that co-worker of yours, are you?"

I shook my head. "No, of course not." I wasn't lying. I'd become more conscious of doing it, since I'd been through a brief phase of thinking I couldn't lie as a result of being a fairy, but that'd just been Blythe sneakily casting spells on me from a distance. *They say the fairies' ancestors weren't able to lie at all,* Alissa had said, so maybe there *was* some truth there, but I was too accomplished a liar to easily be able to give up the habit.

I hesitated before adding, "But I was curious, because hexes are immediate. Curses aren't. So could you put a curse on someone and it wouldn't come into effect until later?"

"In theory—yes. There are two parts. The cast, and the trigger. The cast happens immediately, but the target doesn't necessarily know they have a curse on them. But when the target takes a certain action, the curse kicks in. It can also be put on an object, too."

"That sounds like it'd make it difficult for the victim to tell who cursed them."

"Usually they know who would have done it."

I stifled a sigh. As long as Mr Falconer remained tight-lipped, I was running around in the dark.

"I think we've wandered off topic for long enough," she said, raising her wand in a jangle of bands. "Let's try again."

Half an hour later, I left the witches' headquarters and found Nathan, of all people, outside.

The town's retired paranormal hunter and head security

guard looked more like he modelled for romance novels than chased after paranormal wrongdoers. Dark hair grown a little too long, tall, broad-shouldered, and smiling at me. "Hey, Blair."

"Hey." Great conversationalist, I was not, but I couldn't figure out what he was doing here. "You're not here for magic classes?"

"No, I needed to have a word with Madame Grey about my latest security job. I remembered you had classes, so I decided to see if you were free."

"Ah—why?" I felt my face heat up despite my best efforts to keep my cool. He'd gone out of his way to be nice to me since I'd arrived, and I'd responded by making friends with his mortal enemies. Okay, he and the shifters weren't so much enemies as people who avoided one another. I figured he'd forgiven me for that by now, but things were still kind of awkward between us. On my side, at least.

"It struck me that you haven't seen much of the local scene yet. I guess you've been spending all your time with the witches, but there's a lot more to see."

"Oh—I have," I hastened to say. "Alissa and I went…" I paused. Probably best not to mention the werewolves' favoured haunt in front of someone who didn't get along particularly well with them. "I went to the Laughing Pixie once."

"Oh. I never cared for that place."

"No, I didn't much like it either." Mostly because I'd been there on a 'date' with an undergraduate in a not-so-subtle attempt to get information out of him. Nathan was probably too old for that place, but I was never any good at telling how old people were, and the paranormal element added more confusion. Look at the vampires.

"How about we go to the Troll's Tavern?" He named a pub Alissa had mentioned, but I hadn't been to yet.

"Now? Sure."

Is he asking me out? I'd never been great at reading cues. He *might* be feeling sorry for the newbie again, except he didn't know about Mr Falconer, as far as I was aware.

"I'm not dressed for anywhere fancy," I blurted.

"Do you think I am? It's fine."

His words drew my attention to his jeans, which fit particularly well. My mouth went dry. I definitely needed a drink. At least he wasn't a mind-reader.

The pub, as it turned out, was packed with an eclectic mix of paranormals, thankfully not including werewolves with an over-inflated sense of their own musical prowess. We picked out a spot near a bunch of tables which seemed to belong to some kind of game involving floating balls. Like a pool table, but magical.

"How do you play that?" I asked him. "With a wand?"

"No, they're charmed. We can check it out when one of the tables is free." He returned his attention to the menu, and we both ordered. In most of Fairy Falls's cafes and restaurants, ordering was as simple as tapping what you wanted on the menu and putting your payment on the table. Watching the intense game on the pool tables between a group of teenage wizards helped calm my nerves down. It was a bit ridiculous feeling nervous, but I was not the dating type, and to be honest, neither were the guys I'd been with in the past, either. But I got on just fine with Nathan. If I could avoid melting in front of him like a discarded ice cream.

"You haven't been working for Veronica lately," I commented, taking a bite of pasta. I'd picked something that I wasn't likely to spill or drop. "Is Madame Grey keeping you busy?"

"Yes, she's had some concerns about potential border transgressions between the elves and the shifters."

"Elves?" I echoed. "They live in the forest, right?" I'd never met one, though being fairies, we were technically related. But I already knew my fairy father wasn't an elf.

I also hadn't told Nathan I was half fairy. The only people who knew were Madame Grey, Alissa, Rita, and my boss and co-workers. Okay, that was quite a few people. But after the near-disaster a few weeks ago when Nathan had realised I was lying to him, I'd been wary. Especially since as a paranormal hunter, Nathan had definitely captured and jailed law-breaking fairies.

"Yes," he said. "I'm also spending a lot of time working for a wizard who makes broomsticks and seems to think someone wants to steal them. So I'm watching them for his peace of mind when he isn't at home."

"Is that common?" I asked, recalling Mr Bayer's killer plants which he kept in the garden to stop people from sneaking into his shop and stealing his ingredients. "I mean, do most people who do tricky spells think people want to steal their ideas?"

"Most people? No. Unfortunately, there are some types of magic which are more volatile and dangerous than others."

"Like wand-making," I said casually.

"Yes, like wand-making. Mr Falconer's the only one who can do it, as far as anyone knows."

The only one? I'd known his gift was rare, but not *that* rare. "Have you ever met him? I mean, has he ever asked you to guard his wands, or…?"

I doubted so. The man clearly had his own security measures. Like the wands themselves, for instance. Also, Nathan wasn't a wizard, so he wouldn't otherwise have had reason to visit him.

"No," said Nathan. "I get the impression he thinks anyone who isn't a witch or wizard isn't worth his time."

Hmm. So as much as Mr Falconer had disrespected me, the fact that he'd hired me at all implied he saw my not being a full witch as a non-issue. He'd decided to deny me a wand not out of prejudice, but because he felt like being mean to someone for no apparent reason.

"You're supposed to be applying for a wand yourself, aren't you?" he asked. "Madame Grey said you were almost ready."

I swallowed my bite. "Once I pass my first theory exam. Then I'll be casting spells and hexes left and right."

"I'll remember to duck."

"Ha ha." Apparently, he'd heard enough of my self-deprecation to assume I was okay with him making fun of me.

"Was that too far?" he asked.

"No, it's probably accurate," I said, deciding not to bring up my disastrous wand lesson. "At this rate I'll catch up to the other witches in a few decades... possibly. And that's if I manage not to tick off Mr Falconer. He hired me," I added. "Hired Dritch & Co. I drew the short straw this time."

"He needs another assistant?"

I nodded, chewing another bite. Hmm. He'd said 'don't tell the witches'... not the ex-paranormal hunter. "I'm being coerced into helping him find an employee who doesn't turn into a mouse after a few weeks."

He stared at me a moment. "A mouse? That's why they keep vanishing?"

"Yep."

He looked like he was trying not to laugh. "That's unfortunate."

"You're telling me. And guess who doesn't get a wand until she finds out who did it?"

His expression shuttered abruptly. "What? He can't deny you a wand."

"He can. I'm working for him, and he's the one with the wands. Apparently this is a sort of test."

He shook his head. "Not if it's a problem the wand-maker himself can't solve. It's not a spell, is it?"

"Nope, it's a curse. A powerful one. And he doesn't want me to ask the witches for help, because it'd bruise his ego. They would probably know how to set up the curse, but if it's like a spell, it can only be undone by the person who did it anyway."

He still looked displeased. "Perhaps, but forbidding you to contact allies seems unfair."

"Oh, I'm telling people. Like right now. But as I said, anyone *could* have done it. I'm trying to find out who might have been angry with him a year ago. You were around then, right?"

"Right." He tilted his head thoughtfully. "No, I can't say I spoke to the wand-maker at the time."

"Unless I ask every person in town, I guess I'll have to do this the slow way," I said.

"Who was the first employee to fall victim to the spell?" he asked. "That might give you a clue. He might even have put the curse on himself."

I blinked. "I did consider that. I mean, he seems really mad about it, so I guess he didn't mean to curse the entire job. Just one person. But I don't know. He's a magical expert. Surely he wouldn't do something like that by accident."

"Then he did it on purpose."

"No, he's angry and thinks someone's plotting against him," I said. "He wouldn't keep hiring Dritch & Co to find new people if he did it himself. I'm surprised nobody noticed. I mean, people are going missing and his cover stories are flimsy at best."

"Then perhaps talk to their families," he said. "Maybe one of *them* angered him, or the other way around."

"Hmm." I nodded. "Yeah, that makes sense. I'll get the details of the assistants' families. If they're powerful enough to work as an assistant to the only wand-maker in the town, then I guess their families must be pretty good at magic, too."

Or not, if they'd accidentally got their own relative caught in a spell. But magic could be tricky and unpredictable even to expert spellcasters. Maybe Mr Falconer really had done it himself. It wouldn't be out of character for him to be too stubborn to admit it.

We finished our meals and ordered drinks while Nathan demonstrated the weird floating-ball game.

"You can play with this." He passed me a device shaped like a wand. "Some people use their own wands, but it's set up so paranormals who don't have wands can play, too."

"Seems fair." I twirled the wand in my hand and nearly dropped it. Oops. "So the balls float in the air, and you throw them through the hoops?" There were a series of hoops above the floating table, and it looked like you had to get the balls into the hoops on your opponent's side of the table in order to win. Five balls, five hoops. Seemed vaguely straightforward.

"More or less." He tapped one of them with the wand. It soared to my end of the table, straight through the central hoop.

"Oh, come on," I said, eying the floating scoreboard above the table. "Top score on the first try? That's not playing fair."

He grinned. "Okay, I'll play with my right hand, then. I'm left-handed."

"Somehow I don't think that'll be an issue."

I was right. I lost four games in a row before I managed to score *one* point. The table seemed to be equipped with a kind of force-field so the balls didn't fly across the room whenever I knocked one of them wildly off course. The cocktails were not helpful in this case, though my head buzzed pleasantly by the time we left. Or maybe it was Nathan's close proximity. He was a lot of fun when he wasn't on duty. I had to remind myself not to actually say that, but for once, I'd managed to keep my propensity for putting my foot in my mouth under control.

Nathan walked me home, and my heart rate kicked up as we reached my front door.

"This has been great," I said to him. "Thank you."

"It's my pleasure. I'm glad you liked it."

Small talk was not my thing. Was he going to kiss me goodnight? How did one initiate that type of thing without looking like a fool? I fumbled my keys. Turn around, before or opening the—

"MIAOW."

Several mice pelted through the door, pursued by Sky. Horrified, I didn't stop to think. I ran after them.

"Wait!" I yelled. If Mr Falconer's apprentices got lost out here, they'd be eaten by the local wildlife.

"Blair?" Nathan's tone was perplexed. I didn't blame him. He probably *had* been about to kiss me. Of course, the universe had to upend a bucket of frogs on my head. Or mice. Every one of them had disappeared under the hedge. I swore, then turned to Nathan, figuring I owed him an explanation.

"Sorry. They're not mice," I said, my face flaming. "They ran away from Mr Falconer."

Understanding flared in his eyes. "Oh, they're the former assistants?"

"You've got it. I think my cat knew, before I did, but I don't know why he's randomly chasing them. The other cats here aren't rodent-friendly. But—they might be anywhere."

It was hopeless. It was too dark, even if I did wave farewell to dignity and crawl halfway through the hedge.

"They must understand English," I muttered, dropping to my knees. "Hey—mice!"

Nathan crouched down beside me. "I don't see anything. I think they must have run underneath the fence."

"Oh, no."

I'd yet to meet the neighbours, but most of them would think of rodents as a pest. They might even have mousetraps set up. I got on my knees and leaned underneath the hedge, twigs scraping my forehead. So much for dignity.

Nathan said, "I have a few variants of traps to catch rodents, but they might not work on wizards turned into mice."

I withdrew my head, wincing when a twig scraped my cheek. "The only reason I wanted to help Mr Falconer was because it's unfair that those people have to spend the rest of their lives as mice. And now they're gone."

"I'm sure there's a reason your cat chased them off. Is he your familiar?"

"He thinks he is," I said. "Let's just say we don't really connect. I was seriously confused on the mouse thing until I found out they were human. I thought he was adopting rodents. But maybe he's changed his mind and can't resist chasing them anyway. Cats."

"I have three, so I understand."

Three cats? I could barely handle one.

"Do most of them adopt rodents? Or destroy bubble wrap?"

He raised an eyebrow. "Your cat destroyed the bubble wrap?"

"Yes, I know that's what it was for, but I was having a stressful week and I'd have liked to keep it. Anyway, I realise that's the type of stuff cats do, familiars or not, so I guess I'll just have to hide it next time."

"Right." He nodded. "We'll think of something."

"What, put out a 'have you seen these rodents' sign?" I shook my head. "Sky likes being fed and petted too much to leave for long, so I guess when he comes back, I can ask... I know *he* probably understands English, but he seems selective on whether he responds to me or not. Maybe it's because I'm not... not a fully qualified witch yet."

"I'm told that doesn't usually matter," he said. "But I think you're right about finding them in the dark. I'm sure your cat will come back soon. I'd stay, but I'm actually on guard duty in an hour. But I can stop by on the way back and post a handmade rodent spell through the door?"

"Oh, thank you."

Of course he'd still be working. And I clearly wouldn't be getting a goodnight kiss, even if I wasn't covered in mud and leaves.

"It's okay," I said. "I'll ask Alissa. I'm sure someone will be in."

What an end to our date. But hey, at least it actually *had* been a date.

I entered the flat and switched on the light. No sign of Alissa or Roald. She must have gone out with her co-workers. I sent her a quick message and sat on the sofa, half-heartedly picking a twig out of my hair. At this rate, between the wand-maker, the cat, and the mice, I'd be lucky to get a second date at all.

And where had those mice run off to?

5

I leaned over the hedge, waving the handmade trap. "Here, mousey, mousey…"

"What *are* you doing?" Alissa peered out of the house door, her brow wrinkled in confusion.

I'd woken up the following morning with a new resolution to get this case off my back before it got any more out of hand. Starting with the rodent trap. True to his word, Nathan had dropped it off on the way back from his shift in the early hours of the morning, when I'd been asleep. There hadn't been much point in running around in the dark, so I'd had an early night. Alissa must have come back after I'd gone to bed, which explained her red-rimmed eyes and dishevelled appearance.

By the time I'd got to the end of the story, Alissa was bent double with laughter. She rested her hand on the fence for balance.

"Yeah, it's absolutely hilarious," I said. "Want to help me recover some wayward rodents? How was your night, anyway?"

"Good. The nurses really know how to throw a party

when they're off duty. We have most alcohol poisoning remedies memorised, so everyone wants to party with us. Did you and Nathan kiss?"

"Nope, thanks to that cat. He's still not back, either. Where's Roald?"

She swayed a little as she straightened up. "He was on a date last night. Must have been a good one."

I rolled my eyes. "Even your cat has a more active dating life than I do."

"Hey, you actually got to the date stage this time."

"I also lost my cat," I said. If I couldn't lure the mice back, Sky was a more obvious target, but even leaving a dish of his favourite food outside the door had yielded no results so far.

"Not necessarily," she said. "It's not unusual for him to go out all night."

"It's unusual for him to chase mice off. Who aren't actually mice."

"Let me try."

She ran into the flat, and emerged a minute later holding her wand and a piece of fish. Roald followed, yowling loudly. She waved her wand, then dropped the fish to the floor, where Roald immediately pounced on it.

A moment later—

"You made the whole flat smell of fish?"

"He can't resist," she said. "That, I guarantee."

"The neighbours will be thrilled."

I'd only exchanged a few words with our upstairs neighbours so far. The massive house could fit a dozen families into it, for a massively discounted rate—trustworthy witches and wizards only, thanks to Madame Grey and her slightly blatant favouritism. Not that I was complaining. It was the nicest flat I'd ever lived in—by a mile.

"Also," I added. "I doubt that'll draw the mice back in. You don't think he... might have killed them?"

She pulled a face. "Normally I'd say yes, but I think that cat is more intelligent than we knew."

"Yeah, maybe he had his reasons. I wish we *could* communicate. I've searched the front and back gardens six times, not to mention the rest of the road."

It was the first time I'd ever had a garden and I liked it, but I'd started to wish it was a little less extensive, and with fewer hiding places for rodents.

"He'll be back. I think your cat was just trying to sabotage your date. Or cheer you on. Was Nathan going to kiss you?"

"He was giving kind of mixed signals. Never mind. Clearly I'm destined to be mired in singleness as long as I'm living with that deranged cat."

She grinned. "Does Nathan like cats?"

"He has three."

"There you have it: you're perfect for each other."

"I didn't want *one* cat," I pointed out. "Nor any mice who are actually people. Anyway, we need to find them. Their families are probably seriously worried."

"You're right. Hey, mice!" She waved her wand, and the smell of cheese wafted out. I pressed a hand to my mouth. "Okay, that was a mistake." Her face went slightly green.

"You might as well put *me* in charge." I rolled my eyes. "Couldn't you brew a hangover remedy?"

She giggled. "They only work when you're sober."

Oh boy.

An hour and no mice later, I left Alissa sleeping off the remnants of her night out and went in search of the families of Mr Falconer's previous assistants.

I'd had the presence of mind to bring the files home from work, so I had the names of all the assistants who'd met unfortunate fates. It didn't take too much digging to find out the details of their families, so now I had a plan of action. Starting with the first recorded case of a client he'd hired using Dritch & Co. His name was Oswald Connolly, a member of a prominent wizard family who lived on the other side of town.

Nobody drove here. Cars didn't work around magic, and no one had come up with an effective substitute the way they had with computers and televisions. Since the town had no shortage of broomsticks, transportation spells and my new Seven Millimetre boots, it wasn't impossible to get around, but I sometimes missed modern conveniences. Public transport was admittedly more of an *in*convenience around me, considering how often it broke down. Now I knew it was down to the shield suppressing my magic, not to mention the glamour someone had put on me to hide my fairy side from view. It was weird thinking that I'd been carrying it around all my life, yet knew so little of my real family. Looking at the files—the names, the covens, the details—it seemed clear that everyone knew their own histories, their own families. But I didn't.

I paused outside the small cottage where the Connolly family lived. It was dilapidated, not the manor I'd expect to belong to a prestigious wizard. From the files, he didn't sound like a bad guy. Too bad he was probably hiding from my cat under a bush right now.

What to say to his family? They deserved the truth, but if Mr Falconer kicked me off the job, the curse might never be broken.

A woman in her forties opened the door. "Hello. Can I help you?"

She must be his mother, judging by the information I'd looked up. "I wanted to talk to you about your son," I said.

"You a friend of his?" Her tone was dismissive.

I shook my head. "No." I gathered they hadn't parted on pleasant terms. According to what I'd read, she was a talented witch in her own right. I'd need to tread carefully. "When was the last time you saw him?"

She scowled. "He hasn't come home in almost a year. Why?"

There really was no delicate way to introduce the subject. "I'm actually working with Mr Falconer now," I said. "So, er, I'm looking for previous assistants to speak to, to get an impression of what it might be like to work for him."

"If you've met the man, you'd know. Horrible person. Oswald didn't see it, though. He said he wanted the prestige of working for the town's premier wand-maker. Apparently it was more important than family." She sniffed.

"So he was ambitious?" I asked.

She snorted. "You could say that. He wanted to invent all kinds of things. Wands with built-in special effects, weird nonsense that has no practical use. It didn't do him any good, anyway. Falconer wasn't interested."

No. From what I'd seen of his shop, all his wands looked more or less identical. I'd seen the witches alter their wands after receiving them, adding decorations or different colours, but the basic design appeared exactly the same.

"There are multiplying spells, aren't they?" I asked. "Surely he could just set up a machine, or whatever, and leave it to spit out a hundred identical wands?" Like Lizzie's coffee machine, for instance.

"That's not how it works," said Mrs Connolly. "Those wands may *look* identical, but the magic they contain is unique. A secret known only to wand-makers. Why else would they be able to choose an individual witch or wizard for their own?"

I frowned. "Okay, I didn't think of that. So that's the special magic nobody else can imitate?"

"Obviously," she said. "If Oswald got that far, he never told me. *Secrets,* was the word he always used whenever he called us. And he wouldn't say what. The man made him work fifteen hours a day and barely gave him a moment's peace, but he still acted like he'd been given a solid gold wand."

"So he lived *at* the wand-maker's place?"

"Of course he did. It's a demanding job that leaves no time to visit family, apparently."

A life alone with that grumpy old man sounded like a special kind of hell. Maybe Oswald had turned himself into a mouse to get away from it.

And accidentally cursed the job in the process?

"Did he seem to dislike the job when he spoke to you?"

"Oh, no," she said. "He absolutely loved it. Every call was 'secrets' this and 'classified' that. He dropped all his other interests and didn't talk about anything else during the time he worked for that cantankerous old git."

"He told you secrets?" I asked carefully.

"Oh, he didn't *say* anything," she said. "Never gave a straight answer. I supposed he was under some kind of confidentiality agreement."

Or spell. Wait—was it possible to put someone under a spell not to tell anyone a secret? Most likely... yes. It'd certainly explain why the secrets of wand-making hadn't spread throughout the town.

"So he left—after two weeks?"

"I suppose," said Mrs Connolly. "He called us every few days, but when I didn't hear from him for a while, I began to worry. He wasn't answering my messages, and my calls went to voicemail. So I called the man himself and he said Oswald had left the country. No messages, no traces."

"Did—did you go to the wand-maker's place to check?"

"Of course I did. Nothing there either. By then he had another assistant."

"Did Oswald mention arguing with Mr Falconer?" I asked.

"No," she said. "Worshipped the ground he walked on. Never heard anything like it. The fool. I knew it wouldn't end well for him."

"You did?" I said. "I mean, why?"

"I don't know. Just the way he talked about him. Like he was royalty. And now… I've heard he's had trouble hanging onto an assistant since then."

"You've been there since?"

She nodded. "Three times. He tells the same story every time. Oswald packed up and left town, without another word. Nothing. Not so much as a call." Her voice trembled. "The low-life abandoned his family."

If ever I'd doubted the curse had ruined lives, and Mr Falconer didn't care, I didn't now.

"Yeah," I said. "I—heard there was some issue with the position. With the wand-maker. I'm looking to get to the bottom of it."

"He's alive, isn't he?" she asked.

I nodded. My throat went tight. "Yes. I'm going to do my best to bring him back to you."

I left her house, taking in a deep breath. I'd check *one* more family, and that was it. To find the root of the problem, I'd have to go back further, to whoever Mr Falconer had worked with before he'd first hired Dritch & Co. Because the one common factor was our company. It didn't sound like he and Veronica had a history, so I assumed he'd hired us because we were the only paranormal recruitment firm in town. Nothing weird there. Except that before then, he'd gone after the clients in person, or hadn't had an assistant at all.

That meant there wasn't a trail of evidence if he *had* had an assistant before he'd hired us, unless he opted to tell me himself. In theory, anyone who'd been around for more than a year might know, but it wouldn't do to let too many people guess what I was collecting information for. On the other hand, it was entirely possible that a former assistant of his had been the one behind the curse, out of jealousy or spite. But first, I'd check with another victim's family to see if the cases were as similar as they looked. Just to cover all bases. The former assistants were all people who'd had something to gain by working with him, but none of them had anything to gain from turning his employees into mice. As far as revenge plans went, it was pretty tame.

I walked for ten minutes before I reached the home of the second candidate's family. This one was a fairly nice house with wisteria and ivy growing on the exterior.

A curly-haired pale young woman opened the door.

"Hello," I said. "I'm Blair Wilkes. I'm here to ask you about… your brother."

She grunted. "Went to Switzerland. Never came back. Why?"

"Mr Falconer hired me to find a new assistant and I'm looking into the job history to find the right candidate."

"You won't find him," she muttered. "He won't even call his family." She began to shut the door.

"Wait," I said quickly. "Do you know who was the assistant before he applied? Not Oswald, but—"

"No."

The door slammed. I stood blinking at it. I needed to try another tactic. Surely he must have had another assistant before he'd come to Dritch & Co, and maybe someone knew. But my conversation with Mrs Connolly had reminded me that a customer might easily have been responsible, not an assistant. He sold wands to everyone in town, but as Rita had told me, the majority went to the academy, for the new witches and wizards to receive their wands at the beginning of the school year.

And I'd bet the assistant had been in charge of making that delivery.

The academy was a brick building with its facade embossed with a symbol of two wands crisscrossing. I'd avoided it in the past, since I hadn't wanted to give Rita any ideas about signing me up to take classes alongside a bunch of five-year-olds—not to mention Helen worked there—but at least it meant I knew someone there. And right about now, she'd be in the park next door, setting up the stage for the village fete.

It wasn't hard to spot the stage, because it filled half the park's main field. Magical balloons were tied to the trees, flashing different colours, and flocks of paper birds flew around, to the probable confusion of the local wildlife. Volunteers were spread throughout the park, conjuring up props and setting up the stage. I found Helen behind a stack of cardboard pieces. I assumed someone had waterproofed them, considering rain was forecast all week.

"Hey, Blair!" said Helen, catching my eye. "Did you want to sign up after all?"

"Ah—no, sorry. I've got too much else going on. I wondered... this is going to sound weird, but I'm kind of doing an extracurricular project. For my witch classes. I wondered if we could talk."

She beamed. "Really? That's great!"

"Yeah." I felt bad for lying, and not just because it set off my own inner lie detector. "I wanted to ask about wands. Since I'm getting my own. Who's in charge of ordering the wands?"

"The head-teacher is," she said. "But the other teachers chip in, too. We want the best wands for our students."

"Of course," I said. "How does it work? Do you order the wands in batches?"

"We do," she confirmed. "On the rare occasion that one of our students doesn't connect with a wand right away, we keep trying, and if necessary, we take them to visit the wand-maker in person. Without exception, they always connect with *one* of the wands. Sometimes it takes a little coaxing."

"Mr Falconer strikes me as the type of person who would terrify schoolchildren."

"He is," she said. "But the children are excited enough about getting their own wands that they usually forget about him afterwards."

"And you add the decorations later?" I asked.

"Sure! There's the accessory shop… they sell all sorts of ribbons and other accessories." She waved her own rainbow-painted wand in the air. "You can even change them to another colour."

"But they're all built the same, aren't they?" I asked. "They looked that way, in his window display. Same length, same wood. Wouldn't it be easy for someone else to learn to do the same?"

"Easy? Certainly not," she said. "Mr Falconer has the Magic Touch. He can take an ordinary piece of wandwood and make it unique."

"Wandwood? Er, is that a tree, or…"

"It's a trade secret. They say it's taken from a certain oak tree from the forest. But as I said, the ingredients are nothing on their own. It's the Magic Touch that's the key."

"And can it be taught?" I asked.

"You're not looking to go into wand-making, are you?"

"Nope," I said. "He only wants wizards, for a start."

She blinked. "What do you mean?"

"He's actually hired Dritch & Co to help find him an assistant. He insists only grade five wizards are good enough for him, and I'm having a bit of difficulty finding a suitable candidate. Considering all the wizards either hate him or have some other issue, it's proving tricky."

"Oh, that *is* a situation," she said. "He doesn't like witches? That'd explain why he was so angry when old Ava tried to start her own wand-making business."

Huh? "She did?"

Old Ava was a seer, who'd retired from the coven after losing her marbles, her hair, and possibly her wand, too. At least, she always carried a prop around, as far as I'd heard. I'd spoken to her once, but since Alissa worked at the hospital, maybe she'd know more about her.

"From what I heard, it didn't go well, but he was still pretty angry," Helen went on. "He's the sort who'd get jealous of his own reflection."

I considered this. "But—surely he can't always have been the only wand-maker in town. Someone must have taught him, right?"

"If they did, it was before I was born. As long as I've been here, it's always just been him. He *does* give good discounts to the academy, but that's probably because we're his main source of business. Hmm. I wonder who he'll end up hiring."

Far too late, it hit me that I'd confided in the town's biggest gossip. Except possibly Blythe.

"Wait—don't tell him," I said quickly. "I'm supposed to be doing this job for him this week, but it's confidential. Unfortunately, I also have to apply to him for a wand of my own."

"After you pass your exam, right?"

"Next Friday." I had that long to learn several years of magical theory and figure out who'd cursed Mr Falconer. No pressure, Blair.

"Wow, you *are* busy. If you change your mind about joining us, you know who to contact."

"Sure. Thank you." There was more I wanted to know, but

if I stayed here, I'd end up being mired in extra classes. Or, heaven forbid, dragged into performing on the stage.

I got back home to find a package on the doorstep, addressed to me. A very squishy package, sort of like…

Bubble wrap.

I looked suspiciously around but saw no one. Then I picked up the package and took it into the flat.

"Hey," said Alissa, who sat on the sofa, stroking Roald. "What's that?"

"Delivery," I said, and ripped the packaging off. "Oh, wow."

Her eyes gleamed. "You have an admirer. Let me guess who it is?"

"Don't pretend to be dense. This is just because I mentioned that Sky destroyed my last set of bubble wrap."

"Nathan bought you bubble wrap," said Alissa. "That's the most Blair-specific romantic thing I've ever seen. I should tell him that, if you won't."

I wagged a finger threateningly at her. "Watch it. Don't forget, he doesn't know I'm a fairy yet."

"Still?"

I shook my head. "I'm not ready to tell everyone, but the last thing I want is to find out he doesn't like them, or that he'll think it's a big deal. I know he used to deal with them as a hunter, and not in a pleasant way."

She pulled a face. "I think you're overthinking it."

Maybe I was. I'd started to relax and settle into my new life, but as far as Nathan was concerned… maybe it was nerves about Mr Falconer getting to me.

I shrugged. "Right now, my evil plan is to make him like me as me, then drop the fairy bombshell on him when the time's right."

"He already likes you," she pointed out. "This kind of

secret… it doesn't end well when you knowingly hide something important from someone you're dating."

That's what worried me. I'd had a dozen opportunities to tell him before now, and she was right—we *were* dating. I mean, he'd bought me bubble wrap. That meant he classed me as a friend at least, whether he held me as a potential romantic prospect or not.

"I'll think about it," I said. "Anyway, have you seen Ava lately?"

"Ava? As in, Ava at the hospital?"

"Yep. Apparently, she tried to start her own wand business and argued with Mr Falconer about it."

She blinked. "Er, Blair, Ava has been on the ward for permanent residents at the hospital for over a year. The ward for people who've suffered permanent magical damage."

"Oh. I didn't know. I saw her in the waiting room that one time, so I assumed she came from outside."

"She has a habit of wandering off. She gets confused sometimes. A lot of the time. I wouldn't count on getting straight answers from her. People come in for fortune-telling consults frequently. It annoys the nurses, but she doesn't seem to mind."

Fortune-telling. What she'd said to me hadn't been that, exactly… but she'd all but told me she knew my mother.

"Also," she added, "she hasn't had access to a real wand since her accident. But I can take you there if you're sure she has something to say."

"What exactly happened to her?" I asked.

"She had some kind of backfiring spell incident last year, but she's been showing signs of senility for at least a decade. I doubt this wand-making scheme was anything other than a fantasy of hers."

"It's worth checking out," I said. "It sounds like Mr

Falconer was annoyed at her about setting up a rival business. He's touchy about anyone learning the job."

Which was why his hiring an assistant struck me as kind of weird, but on the other hand, he wouldn't live forever. Wizards and witches weren't immortal. As far as I knew, only vampires were. So he must know he'd have to pass his legendary skills onto someone if he had no children, in order for the wand-maker's shop to remain open.

Alissa nodded when I mentioned this aloud. "Yep. Without him, the witches would have to order wands from outside the town."

"But there *are* places outside the town, right? He must have learnt the business from someone, too."

Her brow furrowed. "Good point. Hmm. I can ask Madame Grey…"

"But she might go and confront him directly, which will only get me into more trouble. Best to speak to Ava first. Then I'll buy you a drink for going into work on a weekend."

She winced. "Please no more cocktails."

6

The other nurses all greeted Alissa warmly, despite their obvious hangovers. This time the waiting room wasn't full of good-looking werewolves, but a bunch of people who'd turned blue.

"Someone's spell went wrong?" I asked Alissa.

"Malfunctioning potion at a house party, I'd guess," she said. "Luckily, it's not my problem today. Let's hope Ava hasn't wandered off again."

"How... I mean, she seemed lucid and pretty coherent when I spoke to her, but is she likely to be able to tell me anything useful?"

"Oh, she's coherent. It's just most of what she says is objectively complete nonsense. She genuinely believes in it, though. And, unfortunately, so do most of the people who come here to speak to a seer."

"Ah."

"I'll find her," she added, walking ahead of me into the ward. I set my expectations firmly at zero, and followed.

Counter to my expectations, the ward for permanent magical injuries did not consist of people in bed or even locked up and muttering to themselves. A man with antlers growing out of his head walked past, while others played chess or sat chatting in corners. I spotted Ava sitting beside a bookcase, her purple wig in disarray and her plastic wand sticking out at an odd angle behind her ear, same as before. She wore a dress patterned with unicorns chasing their tails. It was oddly mesmerising to look at.

While Alissa conversed with a nurse, Ava caught my gaze. "I wondered if I'd be seeing you again, Briar."

"Er, it's Blair," I said. "I hope you don't mind, but I came to talk to you."

She grabbed my arm and yanked me into an empty seat. I'd been heading that way anyway, but her grip was like steel. Ow.

"I can't pretend I didn't see this day was coming," she said.

"Er, do you know why I'm here?" I asked, pulling my arm out of her reach.

"To ask me about your family, of course." Her eyes were bright, eager, and entirely too penetrating.

"You knew my mother," I said, unable to help myself. "You *knew* she was a witch—before I did."

"Of course I did," she said. "Tanith was her mother's protégé, before she ran off. Broke her mother's heart, she did. The poor thing died not long after."

My grandmother. She was talking about my grandmother. "Who… is there anyone still alive? From my family?"

"Here? No. Her father died years ago."

My grandparents were dead? My head spun with a rush of questions, and it took everything I could to drag my thoughts back to the topic at hand. "Er, that's a nice wand." I pointed to the wand tucked behind her ear. "Where'd you get it?"

She looked at me with glassy eyes, her stare a little too intense to hold eye contact with for too long. Perhaps it came with being a seer. She couldn't read minds, but seeing concerned prophecies and other more wishy-washy types of magic. Supposedly, Madame Grey had no patience for it.

"I made it," she said in a conspiratorial whisper.

"Really?" I leaned forward, not having to fake my interest despite the bombshell she'd dropped on me. "That's brilliant. I didn't know you could learn to make your own wand."

She cackled. I'd never heard a witch actually do that since I'd arrived in Fairy Falls.

"Most people can't," she said, her voice still lowered to a whisper. "But I know how."

I let my eyes widen, exaggerating my genuine curiosity. "Tell me more. How did you learn? I've never met anyone who knows how to make wands, so I'm interested. I heard… I heard wandwood is the first ingredient."

"I gathered the wandwood myself," she croaked.

"Where is it from?"

"From the forest, of course. It takes a special skill to find the right trees, but I did it." She laughed again. "I found them, and I made this." She tapped the wand in her hair, and my heart sank. Despite her lucid words, the wand was definitely plastic.

"So this forest… is it near the town?" I asked. Instinct warned me to tread carefully around Mr Falconer's name.

She nodded eagerly. "Of course it is. We get many of our ingredients from there. There are wild magical creatures… plants and herbs that grow nowhere else… it's a protected area of the countryside."

"And you taught yourself to give it the… er, Magic Touch?"

"Who told you that?"

"Nobody. I mean, I just heard that expression. I'm getting a wand of my own this week," I added.

"Don't!" she said loudly. "Don't buy a wand. They're plotting against us!"

Sparks shot from her hand, bouncing off the walls. I jumped. So did some of the other residents. *Whoa. How did she do that?*

As noise erupted around us, I had to raise my voice to be heard. "Why?"

"Because there are no wand-makers left."

I frowned. "Yes, there is." I'd danced around the subject enough. "Doesn't everyone buy from Mr Falconer? Didn't you get your first wand from him?"

"Certainly *not*."

Of course—she and Mr Falconer were both in their seventies, at least. So there must have been someone else who'd been the town's main wand-maker back then.

"Er, so who used to be wand-maker?"

"Mavis Lynch," she said decisively. "Talk to her."

"Okay. I will. I don't suppose you remember—"

"That's enough!" snapped the nurse who'd been talking to Alissa. "I let you in for one discussion, but you've clearly distressed her."

And that was our cue to leave, before they roped Alissa into working on her day off.

"Sorry about that," I said, as we walked out of the hospital. "How *did* she use magic without a wand?"

"She was very powerful before they took her wand. Anyway, did you learn anything useful?"

Where to start? "She does seem to believe she made a wand. She told me to talk to the former wand-maker, Mavis Lynch."

Alissa shook her head. "She's been dead for two decades."

"Oh, no." So much for that. "At least she did say Mr Falconer gets the wandwood from the forest."

"That's not really a secret," she said. "All witches who don't buy or grow their own ingredients get them from the forest. It's accessible to everyone, but I doubt you'll find any clues about Mr Falconer's little issue there. It doesn't sound like the wand ingredients are the problem."

"I know," I said quietly. "But—she said there are no wand-makers left. She also said I shouldn't get a wand and that someone's plotting against us."

"Like I said. Sometimes lucid, but usually makes no sense."

"What happened to her?" I asked. "An accident?"

She nodded. "Her own wand backfired… you know, it wouldn't surprise me if it was connected to her ill-advised attempt to set up her own business. Not that I've ever been able to get answers from the woman herself. Or her family. She has a granddaughter who visits weekly, and that's it."

We picked up sandwiches from the local cafe on the way back, and arrived at the house to find Sky sitting on the doorstep.

I ran up to him. "Sky! Did you bring back the mice?"

"Miaow."

"I've no idea what that means." I also didn't see any mice. "What did you do with Mr Falconer's assistants?"

"Miaow."

"That's helpful." I looked at Alissa. "Great." I was too frazzled to go and relax, and my curiosity refused to be satiated. "Does Ava's granddaughter live here in Fairy Falls?"

"She does," Alissa said. "Annabel Reece. I don't think she inherited as much of the seeing gift as her grandmother did. Ava was living with her when the accident happened, so she might not want to talk about it."

"Oh." I threw the sandwich wrapper in the bin and went to fetch some food for the cats. "Look, doesn't the timing seem weird? A year ago, she tried to set up her own wand-making business. Instead, she ended up putting a permanent spell on herself. What if it wasn't an accident?"

Alissa's face clouded. "That's very illegal, if it's true. But when you mentioned the wand-making business, I did wonder about the timing. I think it's worth talking to her granddaughter. Go easy on her."

"I will." If anything, I had a hundred new questions now. "Where does she live?"

"Goldfinch Lane. Near the forest."

The same forest where wandwood grew? Anywhere was worth a try at this point.

And maybe Ava's granddaughter knew about my parents, too.

———

Ava's granddaughter lived in a pretty cottage that bordered on the thick forest wrapping around the upper side of the lake. The trees grew close together, giving the place a slightly forbidding atmosphere. So this was the forest where the witches gathered their potion ingredients, where the wand-maker worked his magic to extract wandwood from trees... and where Ava had had her accident, not five minutes from her granddaughter's house.

A quick search had told me that Annabel's parents were dead, that she'd been raised by her grandmother and was her only surviving relative, and that she possessed none of the seeing ability herself. I hesitated, then knocked on the door.

A fair-haired young woman with a heart-shaped face answered. There was barely any resemblance between her and Ava, aside from their eyes—both were a startling shade of grey-blue, pale as an autumn sky.

"Hello," I said. "I'm Blair Wilkes, and I—"

"You're the new one my grandmother keeps talking about."

I blinked. "You mean, she talks about me?" So much for having to gently introduce the subject.

"Yes. Whenever I go to see her in the hospital, she always says your name."

Oh... kay. "Er, we only spoke once. She thought I was a seer, but I think she was confused, because I'm not. I think... she knew my mother. Tanith Wildflower." Once again, the barest hint of information on my parents threatened to divert my attention from my mission. But Ava knew *some* things. And while the spell had messed with her mind, her memory seemed to be intact.

Her brows shot up. "I've heard that name, but she talks about a lot of people she used to know. What's she done now? Are you new at the hospital?"

"Ah, no. My friend Alissa works there. But anyway. That's not why I'm here. I heard... she said she tried to start her own wand-making business once. I'm in a situation with Mr Falconer—"

"*Don't* talk to me about that man," she snapped.

Might have been a bit more tactful there, Blair. "My apologies. I'm looking into the history of wand-making and he's not being particularly cooperative. Ava told me she and him had some kind of history."

She heaved out a breath, her eyes sharp and cold. "You might say that. It's because of something *he* said that she got it into her head to go wandering in the forest and hit her head."

"Wait, really? I thought it was a spell."

She shot me a glare. "She was carrying her wand at the time and tried to use it to break her fall. Instead, it backfired. But he might as well have done it."

Her words rang as true to me. She genuinely believed it. But how to bring the topic around to the possibility that the curse was connected?

"Did anyone see what happened?" I asked her. "Including you?"

"I'd know the marks of my mother's own wand," she spat.

"I didn't mean to imply otherwise," I said. But another possibility struck me—what if the town found out their only wand-maker was possibly responsible for casting a permanent spell on one of the town's retired members? That might get ugly.

"I'm sorry," I said, again. "Have you spoken to him since then, or interacted with him in any way?'

"What is this, a questioning? The police already took my statement on the accident."

Hmm. Might *she* have been the one to put the curse on him? If he'd been here, it was definitely possible, but she was already entirely too suspicious of me. According to my lie-sensing ability, however, she'd only told the truth so far.

"I'm new here in town," I explained. "Mr Falconer is insistent that I find him a new apprentice, but I'm hearing less than savoury things about him. I've already had a lot of people turn down the job, so I was wondering if there was something I didn't know. Since your grandmother mentioned his name, I—"

"Didn't anyone tell you not to pay any attention to her rants?"

And she closed the door in my face.

You handled that well. Should I confront the man directly about what he might have done to Ava? If I asked, I'd know right away if he lied.

On the other hand, if things went south, I might end up the next victim instead. I was miles out of my depth, and if Annabel was right, nobody else had witnessed her grandmother's accident. There was no way to prove he wasn't responsible.

As for her attempt at finding wandwood? There was a

path into the woods directly alongside her house. I knew it ended at the lake somewhere, on the other side of the waterfall to the part of the lake I'd been to before. Perhaps I should take to the skies to get my bearings, but while I wore my boots, being able to levitate didn't turn me invisible. I walked down the path, peering over the fence on my left into her slightly overgrown garden. She'd left the curtains partly open. I scanned the room within for anything suspect, but I didn't have a clue what a curse *looked* like. She hadn't lied to me, nor had she given anything away.

I jumped when a faint howl came from the forest. Shifter territory wasn't far away, and while it wasn't the full moon yet, some of them liked to shift into their animal forms to run around the forest. This part of town was wild, unknown, and I hadn't explored it fully yet. With the way I'd accidentally ticked off the werewolf pack in my first week, I was probably best putting that particular task on hold for now. I got lost in my own garden. Wandering into a magical forest without a map fell into the category of 'absurdly reckless decisions'.

Watching from the sky, though? Nope, not reckless at all. Before I could question my wisdom, I switched on my Seven Millimetre boots and levitated above the house, looking down at the trees beyond. From here, I could see how far the territory stretched, but not where the boundaries lay. This part of the forest belonged to the witches, but the unsafe area wasn't clearly marked from this angle. Obviously. *Not your best plan, Blair.*

A strong wind collided with me, blowing me off course and upside-down. Face flaming, and glad nobody was around to witness my latest stunt, I landed gracelessly at the road's end and hoped that the townspeople hadn't looked out of their windows at that particular moment in time. Quite enough adventuring for one day, Blair. Time to go home.

———

No mice waited inside the flat. Roald and Sky did. I tipped cat food into a bowl for Sky, but he turned his nose up at it. "What's the problem this time?"

"Miaow," said Sky.

Roald dove off the sofa and stole his food. "Hey!" I said half-heartedly. Sky didn't take a swipe at Roald, like I'd expected. Still, warring felines were less than a minor problem in my life.

"You didn't eat the mice, did you?" I asked Sky, feeling nauseous at the thought.

"Miaow."

"Where *are* they?"

Sky licked a paw.

I groaned. "Seriously. If they're gone, their families will never see them again. And if they're with Mr Falconer, he's probably the world's worst pet owner."

Alissa came into the room. "What's the verdict?"

"She wouldn't talk to me," I admitted. "I upset her by bringing up the subject. I know, I know, I shouldn't have, but I'm starting to think we were right—Mr Falconer definitely argued with her, before the accident. Which would give her a motive to teach him a lesson. I looked around, but I don't even know what a curse looks like, so I wouldn't have known if she set it up."

Alissa took a seat next to me on the sofa. "He argued with her? Both her and Ava? I wish I knew how to get straight answers out of Ava, but the best paranormal doctors on the planet can't get through to a seer who's lost her senses."

"Annabel definitely seems to blame him," I said. "I mean— it's awful if it's true, but what if he *was* responsible for her accident? Even if it wasn't deliberate, look what he did with the mice. It'd be just like him to refuse to face up to it."

She shifted to the side when Roald squeezed his way between us on the sofa and stretched out. "Are you sure she didn't give anything away?"

I petted Roald. "I wish I'd been more delicate with my questioning. She brought up my mother and it threw me off. Anyway, it's possible this grudge started before the accident."

Sky nudged the back of my head. *Speaking of grudges.* I didn't like the look he gave Roald, so I lifted him into my lap before he took it upon himself to dive on top of the other cat and steal his spot. It'd been known to happen.

Alissa said, "That wouldn't surprise me, given how long both of them have lived here. Tell you what, I'll speak to Ava again. If I mention your name, she's bound to pay me some attention. What would you like me to ask her?"

About my mother. No—not that. "For a start, I'd like to know if she did speak directly to Mr Falconer. If he went to her house. Because she might have cursed him while he was there. Or Annabel did. If the curse hit him after the accident, she wouldn't have had a wand, right?"

"You know—yes, you're right," she said. "The thorny issue is that curses are possibly the trickiest type of magic there is. And this one has never been done before. It's obvious that Ava—and possibly her granddaughter—definitely have the imagination to come up with a curse like that, but not necessarily the skill. Especially Ava. I'd be more inclined to believe Annabel did it, but she's not that skilled at magic."

Hmm. She was the most likely person, and the facts fit. Ava had seemed genuinely distressed when she'd talked about Mr Falconer, but I hadn't spent long enough around her to know if that was typical behaviour for her or not. At the same time, her words had resonated and hadn't set off my inner lie detector. Maybe it was because I had a soft spot for the underdog, and it sounded like seers were it, in the eyes of the other witches at least. Paranormals seemed to grow more complicated the more time I spent here, and I still had that outsider's perspective that I wasn't sure would ever go away.

Alissa said, "Lots of people keep secrets. It's not that uncommon. It's why when stuff like this happens, it goes unnoticed."

I stroked Sky, and he purred contentedly. "I do think Annabel was hiding something. She lives right next to the forest."

She rolled her eyes. "Let me guess—you went snooping."

"Don't worry, I didn't go inside. I was just curious about the wandwood. And I was told witches use the forest to gather ingredients all the time."

"Didn't you end up being ambushed by killer plants the last time you went wandering somewhere without permission?"

Touché. "Yes, but this time I don't have to sneak around. The forest is public property."

"Technically, it's the witches' property."

"Isn't basically everything their property? Our house is. So is the office where I work, the garden, the high street..."

She sighed. "I won't stop you. But avoid the part past the row of trees that have no bark on them. That's shifter territory. It's fairly well marked out, but be on your guard."

"I'll keep that in mind."

The weather was still dodgy enough that I didn't quite want to risk using the boots again... but I still had some options. I'd just take a quick look. That was all.

———

This is a bad idea. I had no sense of direction. The forest didn't have a map. And there might be dangerous magical creatures wandering around.

What I *did* have was a pair of fast, levitating shoes, and an insatiable curiosity which had kept me up all night. So here I was, at five in the morning, walking to the far end of town where the lake merged with the forest. Birdsong mingled with the distant sound of the waterfall, growing louder as the houses became more spaced out. The witches used the paths so often, they'd left a well-worn track leading into the thick forest, which I followed.

The trees closed over my head immediately, and the lightening sky suddenly seemed a long way off. Eerie silence pervaded, and grey mist clung to the low-hanging branches.

What are you even looking for in here?

Not wandwood. I doubted I had the skill to make wands, nor did I particularly want to. No… Annabel had said her grandmother's spell had backfired in a clearing not far from here. If I found it…

What did I expect? The wand she carried was a fake. She might never have created one at all. But she'd believed she had, and that was enough for my lie detecting ability.

As for my second purpose…

I pulled out the guide to plants I'd borrowed from Rita, crouched down and picked a few leaves. I'd looked up the recipe for an invisibility potion—a tricky potion, and definitely not one I'd be using in class—but it might help me get answers from Mr Falconer if he refused to talk. I'd wait and see what I could find out in the meantime.

Three clearings later and I stopped abruptly. Two trees had fallen so they stood at right-angles to one another. The rest of the clearing was bare of life. Dead trees. No birdsong. Just the scorched remains of a backfiring spell. I could smell its bitter tang in the air.

"What are you doing here?" a small, shrill voice demanded. It belonged to a man considerably shorter than I was, with pointed ears, pale skin, and clothes the colour of the surrounding forest—which explained why I hadn't seen him a foot away from me.

I jumped. "Hi."

Goblin? No... elf.

"You look lost," he said, his teeth bared in a grin. "Come to find the cursed clearing?"

"Is that what it's called?" My heart began to beat faster.

"So we say. A terrible curse was cast here, and it damaged the forest."

"I—really?" I said, surprised into feigning ignorance. Nathan had mentioned something about elves causing trouble, but I couldn't recall him saying how. "Isn't this the witches' forest?"

His mouth twisted. "They were rotten to the core, the people who cut down the forest and turned our trees into weapons. And you, too."

"I'm not," I said, holding up my hands. "See? No wand. I'm new in town and thought I'd have a look around. So, er, what's wrong with the wands?" Why did everyone seem to want me to *not* have one?

"It's unnatural. Their magic. Wands are human creations," he growled.

Okay...

"I have no idea what you're talking about," I said. "Do you have a problem with the person who made the wands?"

"The human with the devil's touch," he hissed. "Evil man."

"Wait, it was him, then? Did you—"

Before I could finish my sentence, the elf had disappeared into the forest.

Hmm. He seemed to have some kind of grudge against the wand-makers—a fact that would normally land him on my suspect list. But he'd also sounded like he hated witch magic, curses included—assuming he hadn't been trying to creep me out.

Weird. Definitely weird.

I got back home to find Alissa waiting outside the house. "I was about to come after you," she said.

"Not to worry," I said. "Who would I talk to if I wanted to learn about the elves?"

She blinked sleepily. "The *elves?*"

"They had some kind of dispute with the witches," I said. "And have a huge grudge against the wand-makers, particularly Mr Falconer."

Her brow furrowed. "You're saying an elf set up the curse?"

"I have no idea. They do have magic, right?"

She nodded. "Nature-based, mostly. They can make things grow… and that's about it. They affect things like the weather, too, but on a less volatile scale than weather-witches or similar. Otherwise, they're probably not responsible for the curse. If he'd angered the elves, he'd be dealing with sour milk or itchy… parts."

I smothered a laugh. Still, they had reason to be annoyed with him, given how overprotective they apparently were of the forest. "He seemed incredibly ticked off, the one I spoke to. Is there someone else, an elf who's more… friendly with humans? I think it's worth looking into."

"To be honest, I don't think any of them are friendly with humans," she said. "Madame Grey dislikes them, but she never went into any detail about why. I guess it's because the witches and the elves have always argued over the forest."

"Sounds about right." I never thought not having a wand might actually be an advantage, but it'd probably saved my neck out there. Though the elf hadn't exactly struck me as dangerous, it seemed pretty clear to me that there was something going on in the wand-making business that went far beyond a few mice.

7

The first thing I encountered at work on Monday morning was an angry voicemail message from the man himself. Steeling myself, I dialled his number.

"Wilkes," he growled. "Have you found any suitable candidates yet?"

"I haven't," I said. "I did look around over the weekend, but I haven't yet found another candidate."

I emphasised the word *weekend,* though his annoyance was the least of my worries. How was I supposed to get on the topic of how he might have hurt an innocent woman—much less damaged the witches' forest and caught the ire of the elves who lived there?

"Stop wasting my time," he growled. "This is your job."

"I'm aware of that. I've spoken to dozens of potential assistants on your behalf, but none of them is available to apply. You've been through so many people that it's difficult to find new candidates."

"Does that include Arabella Connolly? Don't think I didn't hear about you snooping around."

"You—" *He was spying on me?*

"The stupid girl called me this morning. She seemed convinced I know where her son is."

"Well," I said, "you do."

There was a slight pause. "I can't tell one candidate from another."

Huh? Oh—he meant the mice. "That's not her fault," I said, "I spoke to her because I thought he might have been linked to the curse—"

"Don't speak of that over the phone," he growled. "Come to me in person if you wish to discuss confidential matters."

My heart jumped into my throat. "That won't be necessary. I'll call up some more candidates, but you should know you aren't my only client. I spoke to the family of the last one because they might have known if your previous assistants had some personal issues with you. Unless you have anything else you'd like to disclose yourself?"

"Only that I sincerely regret hiring you, Miss Wilkes, and unless you want to be without a wand, you'll do your job."

Despite my growing apprehension, a sliver of indignation peeked through.

"Isn't that blackmail?" I asked. "You told me not to report you to the witches, but you're technically breaking the law by forcing me to work outside the limits of the job description. It's not like we signed a contract—"

He hung up.

Bethan arched her eyebrows at me. "You're treading on dangerous ground."

"He's being deliberately unhelpful." And he'd brought the curse on himself, that much was abundantly clear. I was seriously tempted to tell the others, my boss included, but if the worst of the stories was true, he was dangerous, more so than I'd guessed from dealing with him in person. But the spark of my anger had well and truly ignited. I rage-sorted files for several minutes, fuming silently.

"Boss incoming," muttered Bethan.

A moment later, Veronica entered the office, and she walked to my desk.

"I just heard from Mr Falconer," she said. "Apparently you've yet to find him an assistant."

"The person I picked quit before getting to the job," I explained. "His demands are a bit more excessive than any other client. There's a limited number of possible candidates."

"I know he's unpleasant to work with, but he could muddy our name with everyone in town," she said. "I have to ask you to turn your attention to the job immediately. If this goes south, he could easily prevent us from getting any more clients. He also told me to reiterate that nobody except you knows the precise details of your job, and to tread carefully or else those details might make their way back to your mentor."

Whoa. The crafty git was implying he'd blame *me* for the curse? Now that was underhanded.

"How did *he* end up being the only person in town who can create new wands?" I asked. Oops. I probably should have modified my tone before I spoke to the boss.

"He's lived here longer than I have, so I'm not the person to ask," Veronica said. "But when it comes to specialist areas like wand-making, it takes a type of skill that can't be demonstrated. Like Mr Bayer's handmade spells. If any person tried to copy them, they wouldn't succeed. It's to do with innate magical talent."

The Magic Touch. But Mr Falconer had given so little away about the process, I had to wonder what exactly he was teaching his apprentices.

Hang on a moment. It didn't sound like Mr Falconer was checking whether his applicants had the talent or not before teaching them. So it must be possible to teach that skill. Right?

Before I could ask, Veronica said, "Find him someone—anyone will do—and get him out of our hair."

That was the plan. If not for the twenty former assistants who were still stuck as mice, and Ava possibly being his victim.

I nodded. "I'll do my best. But—"

"Believe me when I say the man is not to be underestimated. We're a small business. He's the foundation of the town's entire source of magic."

And she swept out of the office, leaving me gaping after her. *He's what?* Wands were important, there was no disputing that, but they weren't absolutely essential. Right? The elf had implied as much, though to be honest, this morning felt like a bizarre dream. And in Fairy Falls, that was saying something. As for what Veronica had said? I didn't particularly want to know what damage a man with hundreds of wands could do. Hold the whole town hostage, even. He had that much power, even though people disliked him.

Was that the so-called Magic Touch?

———

My head was in the clouds for the rest of the day. I nearly forgot my magic lesson after work, and had to sprint to the witches' meeting place.

I burst into the classroom, where to my relief, Rita hadn't left yet.

"Sorry I'm late," I gasped, falling into a chair in the front row.

"I heard you were busy over the weekend," she remarked. "You were seen near the forest this morning, too."

My heart sank. "By who?"

Bangles clattered as she pulled out her wand. "There's no need to look so alarmed. A lot of witches use the forest, but Helen was concerned you might have got yourself lost in there."

Of course. Better Helen than, say, Madame Grey, but it figured she'd report me to the other witches. *I guess Mr Falconer wouldn't necessarily assume I was in there looking for clues about the curse.* Just as long as she hadn't seen me near Annabel's house.

"I heard it's where the witches get their potion ingredients, so I got curious." Lucky I *could* lie, though it might have been better for everyone if I'd permanently lost that ability after all. "Anyway, I ran into an elf. He seemed pretty ticked off about my being there, even though it's the witches' forest, right? I thought only the shifters lived in the woods."

"They own a section of the forest, yes," said Rita, taking up her position at the front of the room. "And the elves own another section. Unfortunately, they have a habit of trying to extend their territory. They see the entire forest as theirs. We've had a contentious history with them, the witches have."

I'd bet a certain wand-maker hadn't helped.

"You have?" I asked, curiously. "What have they done?"

"The elves are notorious pranksters," she said. "We had to set up clear boundaries, otherwise they'd sour the milk and put things in the water supply."

"That sounds… malicious."

She grunted. "The witches who lived near their former territory were no better."

"Were?" I echoed. "It must have ended somehow, if you leave one another alone now."

"It's been fairly quiet for years," she commented. "There

was never an open conflict. The elves gradually withdrew over the years, and this is the result."

Hmm. They'd certainly have a reason to be angry with Mr Falconer, if a misguided one. On the other hand, elves couldn't curse people. Only witches or wizards could. So unless someone who had too much sympathy for slightly crabby beings who hated humans—enough to screw up other humans' lives—then I couldn't see the elves being linked to the curse.

"Are they normally hostile when they run into you in the forest?" I asked. "He seemed to think my being there was ruining the forest and he said wands are evil witch props made for nefarious purposes, or something like that."

"I've heard that one before," she said. "It's a common line of theirs that the forests are for the elves and anyone who uses them for any other purpose is selfish. The fact is, though —we grew the forest ourselves. They moved in later and decided to try to claim it as their own territory. While we let them have part of it, since there are so few magical forests left in England, they weren't originally there. It's humans— normals—who did most of the damage."

I turned this over in my mind. "What about the wand-wood? He seemed particularly annoyed about wands. Said they caused damage."

"Certainly not," she said. "Don't let their crafty manner and reasonable words fool you. They are notorious for tricking humans, and most of the contact we get from the paranormal police department concerning cases where normals have been bewitched involve the elves in some way. That forest has always belonged to the witches."

I nodded. "So—how is their magic different to ours? He said his magic was real and ours wasn't."

She snorted. "Hardly. The elves' magic is connected

directly to nature in a way ours isn't. It's not better or worse, it just is."

"Are fairies—like me, are we related to the elves?"

"You're in the same paranormal class, but that would be like comparing a human to a cat. Both mammals, vastly different in almost every way."

I should hope so, considering my own recent experiences in the pet department.

My 'real' un-glamoured form had pointed ears and wings. I hadn't got a look in a mirror when I'd stepped under the waterfall—Fairy Falls—to take the disguise off. And as easy as it'd been to switch it back on at the time, I hadn't returned to the falls since. I didn't feel the slightest connection what-soever with the elf I'd run into in the forest, and he hadn't seemed to recognise me as one of the fairies. I couldn't imagine spending my time lurking in forests to terrify people, or pranking humans for fun.

Never mind the elves. I was certain Ava's accident was linked with Mr Falconer, but the way even my boss implic-itly trusted his ability didn't sit right with me. The more I dealt with him, the more I suspected there was more at play than a deficit of witches and wizards with wand-making talents. But could I really unravel the situation myself, with no wand of my own?

———

When I left my lesson, I nearly collided with a figure who appeared outside the door as suddenly as a gust of wind on a clear day. He wore dark clothes, possibly to hide bloodstains, and had pointed teeth and pale skin along the lines of a waxwork model. Vincent the vampire was the oldest resident of Fairy Falls, by a few hundred years, and had apparently spent several of those years perfecting the art of sneaking up on people.

"Blair Wilkes," he said. "Here for a magic lesson?"

"I—yes, I am." I never felt entirely at ease around the guy. Probably because he drank human blood, even if it did come from the blood donations at the local hospital and not through the jugular. He'd also given me his business card once, as a direct challenge to a group of werewolves who didn't like me much. Supposedly, I was meant to pick one side over the other, but I tended to just avoid both of them. On the other hand… "I was actually looking to talk to someone about town history."

"Were you really?" he asked.

Until about five seconds ago, nope. I'd heard a rumour that vampires could read minds, but surely he hadn't been waiting for me. For reasons I couldn't fathom, he spent a great deal of time hanging out in the history section of the local bookshop. Apparently he had memory issues after living such a long time, which meant he might not be able to answer my questions, but it was worth a try.

"Okay, so I was talking to Ava," I said. "You know, the seer."

"Oh, her. I'm frankly surprised people still go to her for prophecies, considering she didn't foresee her own fate."

"That's not nice to say. You're immortal." And a complete—

"Careful, now."

I took a step back. "You *are* reading my thoughts." And I thought I'd seen the end of that when Blythe left Dritch & Co.

He tilted his head. "Does that make you uncomfortable?"

"Obviously. How long have you been doing that?"

"I merely get impressions when you're particularly… agitated."

Is that supposed to make me feel reassured? I pushed down the thought. "If that's the case, you probably know what I want to ask you."

"No, I can't say I do. You went to see the old seer, like so many before you."

I frowned. "She gives out prophecies that often?"

"Fairly often, yes. She's the only living seer in the town, despite her condition."

And there I was thinking I was getting special treatment. "Right. I wondered… did you ever know Mavis Lynch? The former wand-maker?"

"That's too recent history," he said, in a disappointed tone. "There are better centuries. I could tell you about the fifteen-hundreds."

"Er, that sounds interesting," I said. "But I wanted to know more about wand-making. Was it always such a closely guarded secret?"

"Yes," he said. "Since I'm not a wizard, I know nothing of it."

Lie.

His gaze sharpened. "That is a remarkable gift you possess."

"Now you're reading my witch skill?"

Why did I think it was a good idea to talk to him? Why?

"You ask of wand-making. I do recall an incident a few decades ago, in which a large number of wand-makers retired from the craft at once. I believe there was memory loss involved. The craft has always been restricted to a single coven, and the elders died without ever passing on their knowledge."

I became aware my jaw was hanging open and closed it. "They all forgot? All of them? Who?"

Wow. What *had* Mr Falconer done?

"Yes, they did, or so they say," he said, sounding bored at

the very thought. "I can't say I know what the issue was. Perhaps they tired of the craft."

"You just said they lost all memory of the craft. Did they do that themselves?"

"I often wish I could forget," he said. "Perhaps this is my punishment."

"Save your brooding," I said. "You're seriously saying that an entire coven of witches *forgot* the craft of wand-making?"

"You exaggerate. There were never many who knew it. Four or five at most."

"And somehow Mr Falconer is the only one left?"

"I suppose he is."

"And everyone uses his wands, without questioning why nobody else makes them?"

"Questioning?" he echoed. "It was decades ago. Fifty years, at least, which is not, I believe, relevant to your task."

"Task… can you please stop doing that?"

Ignoring me, he added, "And yes, the younger generation use his wands. The older ones do not."

"And some of us might not get one unless we find him an apprentice," I finished. "You knew that, didn't you? You read it from my thoughts the moment you saw me. And you—you must have known the truth all along. What really happened when Ava tried to become a wand-maker?"

He regarded me with that oddly still face, blank of emotion. "The truth is, I don't know. Old Ava's thoughts are jumbled and she has some fairly vivid delusions. The most frequently recurring memory of the event matches the public story."

My heart sank a little. Could my ability distinguish truth from lie when the other person honestly believed they were telling the truth? Where was the limit?

"Have you at any point read anything in anyone's head about a curse?" I asked.

"Not that particular curse, no. Curses don't personally interest me. I prefer more *direct* ways of dealing with my enemies."

He smiled, and his fangs were a little too prominent. I resisted the impulse to back away—with vampire speed, he could catch up to me in approximately four seconds.

"It's been a pleasure talking to you, Blair."

And he vanished, swift and quiet as a ghost. I stared after him. What had he come here for, then? Probably, when it came to vampires, I didn't want to know. But I did need to get the witches' version of the story. Would Rita know? Maybe she would, and yet…

The doors to the lobby opened and Alissa came in. "Is something wrong? I saw that vampire leaving…"

"Oh, it's fine," I said. "I was just asking him about the history of wand-making. Is your grandmother around?"

"Not at the moment."

"Did you know the witches who used to create wands lost their memories?"

She blinked. "No. Was that what you and the vampire were talking about?"

"Yes. He doesn't remember it very well, but he's convinced that the coven who used to hold all the secrets of wand-making suddenly forgot all about it. Decades ago."

Her brow furrowed. "Sometimes his memory is as dodgy as Ava's, so I wouldn't take his word for it."

Hmm. If wand-making came with the risk of losing one's memory, I wouldn't be keen either. Never mind turning into a mouse. "Where is Madame Grey? I really need to ask her about this."

"She's at chess club."

Everyone had more of a social life than I did. "Might she have left her office open?"

She gave a firm head-shake. "No, she always locks the door. And Rita has the only spare key."

I groaned. "You know, I'm wasting my time. The most likely place to find answers is in the hands of the man himself. Does he never leave the shop at all? Except when he goes into the forest and annoys the elves? Wait, how often does wandwood need to be gathered? Someone mentioned the full moon…"

She gave me an eye-roll. "You know that's when all the shifters take on their animal forms and lose all memory of their human selves, don't you?"

Ah. "Don't worry, I need to solve it before next week, otherwise I can say goodbye to any chance at getting a wand. I just want to see what he's hiding in the shop. He must have evidence he's hiding from me."

Her expression turned calculating. "You know… there *is* another possibility. I can brew a transportation spell."

Of course. "That's a much more practical idea." More so than my attempt to gather ingredients for a tricky invisibility potion.

"Not that I'm trying to encourage breaking and entering. But he's always out in the forest in the evenings. Every single day, rain or shine."

"Wait, he is? I thought he and the elves hated each other."

"I've no idea what he does in there," she said. "But he's often in the forest all night. I think this is the best shot you have."

"I agree. I can't get him to admit who was his assistant before this curse kicked off. Unless it *was* Ava, or her grand-daughter, but I can't get through to either of them. How easy is it to make that transportation spell?"

"Not too hard," she said. "It requires a few props. But I can help."

"Thanks," I said, gratefully. "I've tried the human route. I think it's time to try the magical one. Unless I can put *him* under a spell to spit out the information?"

Alissa's brow wrinkled. "No spell will work on him. He'll notice, or those sentinel wands of his will. No… the best bet is probably to sneak in. Much less risky."

"Let's hope so."

8

———————

With Alissa's steady hand guiding the process, putting the spell together was relatively simple. I felt vaguely foolish standing on the floor of an empty classroom surrounded by leaves interspersed with various herbs, but she was confident the transportation spell would get me right into Mr Falconer's back room. Then all I needed to do was poke around. And not get caught.

Alissa was certain that he wouldn't be present, but my luck had taken a severe downturn lately. My nerves spiked as she pointed her wand at the circle of leaves.

"Make sure you keep your attention on the room," she said. "Don't let any other thoughts in."

"Got it," I said. "Just get it over with. I'll be back when the spell runs out." The spell wasn't likely to be comfortable, but options were limited.

I held the image of the shop in my head, as clearly as I could, and—

Bang.

My head cracked off stone. I groaned, rolling across rain-wet earth. Ow. I hadn't landed inside Mr Falconer's shop, but outside it. Either the spell hadn't been precise enough, or his shop was spell-proof. I'd bet my non-existent wand on the latter. In fairness, it *had* been a long shot. I picked bits of leaf out of my hair and rubbed mud from my face, smearing it down my neck in the process. It was the second time that week that I had reason to be grateful that there were no witnesses around.

Wait a moment. Maybe I'd be able to find those missing mice. I trod carefully down the side of his shop, looking under the hedge.

"What are you doing?" Mr Falconer demanded, emerging from the bushes like a particularly solid and angry ghost.

Oh no.

"I was looking for the mice," I said innocently.

"You know where the bloody mice are."

"Not all of them." I took a step backwards away from his glare. "A few of them showed up at my house, before you hired me. They ran away. I thought they might have come back here, so I wanted to check. If we undo the curse and the mice are gone, they won't be able to turn human again. There's no way into your shop, so I thought they might be outside."

"You thought wrong." He shook his head. "You're pathetic. Feeling sorry for those idiotic creatures?"

"They're *people*," I pointed out. "And your curse got them stuck like that. I thought you wanted to set them free."

His fists clenched, and sparks shot from the wand I belatedly noticed he had clenched in his right hand. "They were all disappointments in the end. I want this curse off my job so I can hire a *real* apprentice who won't make a complete mess of things."

I took another step backwards, one eye on the sparking wand. "Is that what you think they did? All of them? I wouldn't have thought they'd have had the chance to do much before the curse took hold. Weren't they just getting started?"

He stepped in closer, his eyes narrowed. "It's none of your business."

I folded my arms across my chest to hide my shaking hands. "You can't expect me to find the truth if you withhold vital details. What do you teach them in the first two weeks of the job? Maybe that's what's causing it."

"Are you accusing me of cursing my apprentices?"

Possibly. He was as likely a suspect as anyone, but if anything, I thought Ava or her granddaughter was the most likely culprit. At the same time, I couldn't suppress my curiosity about the previous wand-makers.

"No," I said to him, "but you have to admit that since you haven't told anyone aside from me, the evidence makes you look as guilty as the other possible perpetrators. And as I said, I need all the information possible if I'm to come to an accurate conclusion. I'm not a mind-reader or a qualified detective, for that matter, so if that's what you're looking for, you hired the wrong person."

"And the fact that you worked out who killed Mr Bayer was pure luck?"

"Well," I said. "Yeah. It kind of was." My knees shook, but I stood up straighter. "I've been doing my best to find you a suitable candidate, Mr Falconer, but frankly, I don't know what to tell the people who seem convinced that you're doing this to your candidates yourself. Not when it's plausible to anyone who doesn't know the full story." *Including me.*

He hissed out a breath. "For your information, I did *not* curse my own candidates. If I wanted to punish them, I have a number of more immediate and effective weapons present right here. A curse like that is tame by comparison, if I were capable of casting one. Which I'm not."

He spoke the truth. That meant… not only had he not cursed the job, there was a type of magic he couldn't do after all. Curses didn't require wands, but it would have been so much simpler if he *had* done it.

Or not, considering the town would be without a wandmaker if he wound up in jail.

"I had to ask, because several people are already concerned," I said. "They also seem to think you did something to anger the witches and that's why they won't work with you."

His face reddened. "I told you not to tell anyone."

"I didn't. But people talk. Are you certain a witch or wizard did it? There are a lot of witches and I've only met a few of them in the short time I've lived here."

"That is not my problem," he growled. "Any of them might have done it."

"Then what about Ava?" My body tensed, ready to run.

"Ava?" he echoed.

"You know. The town seer. She's currently in hospital—the same hospital Alissa works at—and I've run into her a few times. Anyway…" I faltered. What if I misjudged and got her hurt? I didn't want to put anyone else in the path of Mr Falconer's anger.

"What about her?" he asked.

"She was raving about creating her own wand," I said. "Seemed insistent on it. She was also raving about a bunch of other stuff, but the nurses said that one came up a lot. And—apparently she was injured in the forest not long afterwards."

"Isn't that a pity?" he said, in a soft, deadly voice. "I heard the rumours, and I will say that I did nothing to that old woman. She brought it on herself with her meddling."

My throat went dry. "You—did you cause Ava's… accident?"

"Certainly *not*," he said. "She was losing her wits long

before she started that ill-advised attempt to gather wand-wood. It wouldn't have done her any good, anyway. She was never trained by a wand-maker."

His words didn't register as lies. My heart continued to gallop in my chest, but I could breathe easier—even if I did have twice as many questions. "I heard—the last wand-makers lost their memories. Is it true?"

"I didn't call you here to discuss town history," he growled. "I didn't call you here at all. You're trespassing."

"Technically, I'm in the road, not your shop," I pointed out, probably unwisely. "Don't you find it odd that a whole coven lost their memories?"

"You clearly have a great number of gaps in your education," he said. "Ask the witches if you must insist on satiating your curiosity, but the past has no bearing on whoever cursed my job. It happened decades ago. The curse came into effect last year."

Right. "Just thought it weird that there's only one wand-maker, that's all. Seems a lot of pressure to put on your apprentice, too."

"Precisely why I only want the best," he said. "If it *is* that seer, blaming me for her ailments, I'll see to it that the police set her straight."

You evil old man. Could you actually get arrested for putting a curse on someone's job? I hadn't seen enough of the paranormal rulebook to make a judgement call on that one. After all, even if she was responsible, Ava was hospitalised with a serious injury. That ought to get her off the hook. Right?

"I don't think it's her," I said, ineffectually. "She's injured, anyway."

"Not my concern. Anyone who threatens my business pays. And that includes you, Blair Wilkes."

Alissa waited for me when I hurried breathlessly back into the classroom—the spell had fizzled out when I'd bounced off whatever defences Mr Falconer had around the shop, so I'd had to run back to the witches' place with my face and neck covered in mud. "I was about to send out a search party."

"It didn't work," I said, letting the door swing shut behind me. "He has some kind of shield around his place, and I bounced straight off it. And on top of that, he caught me outside, and I don't think he entirely bought my excuse that I was looking for those mice."

Her eyes widened. "Oh no. I really didn't think he'd be there. You got away lightly, I think."

"No kidding. Anyway, he's still refusing to say what he actually teaches his apprentices. He insists it's not relevant. But there is this—I got him to say directly that he didn't put the curse on the job himself. And my lie detecting ability didn't go off. He was telling the truth. On the other hand, I accidentally alerted him to the fact that Ava might have done it. He says anyone who threatens his business will spend the rest of their lives in jail."

Her expression went steely. "He can try. Trust me, the nurses won't have any of it, and even the police wouldn't arrest someone from the ward."

"Have you seen her today?"

She nodded. "She's given a grand total of twelve false prophecies this week already. The staff will never believe his accusations. Even if they're true. She's been leading people astray for years."

I heard the implied meaning—she might not have known my mother at all. But she'd seemed so sure. This was where it'd come in handy to properly understand my ability to sense lies. Because if it did kick in when the other person believed what they said was true even if it was complete nonsense, there was no point in putting my trust in it to solve this case. Not to mention, it was typical that the one person willing to talk to me about my mother was possibly delusional.

"Seeing is rarely accurate, even if your mind is clear," Alissa explained. "Because you get visions of the past and future at once. It can get overwhelming."

"I guess so. Mr Falconer didn't seem to think he was responsible for her accident, but I don't know. It seems odd that he spoke to her at all."

Her brow wrinkled. "So did he give you any clues?"

"Nope. He wouldn't back up what Vincent said about the last wand-makers losing their memories. Unless I corner Vincent again to ask for the name of someone living who might be able to help, but at this rate, he's going to think I'm using him for his historical knowledge."

"Or that you like him. Which won't bode well for your relationship with Nathan." She winked.

"There is no relationship. I haven't even seen him all week thanks to Mr Falconer, work, and the exam I'm going to completely fail at this rate." I hadn't even touched my revision notes since Mr Falconer had given me the job.

Her gaze filled with sympathy. "I could ask for Madame Grey to pull you out?"

"Nope," I said firmly. "I'm not putting this off. I just haven't organised my time as well as I should have." Since I kept sneaking off into forests or trying to get into Mr Falconer's shop instead.

"Hey, you've had a lot on your mind. I'm surprised your boss is still pressing you to help Mr Falconer, given his history. Maybe he's bribing her?"

"No, that… doesn't sound like Veronica. Maybe he's Simeon's relation and is using mind control, too."

"Nope," she said. "I checked if anyone else in the town has that power, afterwards, and he isn't one of them. And Blair hasn't been anywhere near him. She's under close watch, with her wand bound."

I stowed that information away. "Maybe he's manipulating people… he's definitely not doing anything to me, though. Aside from blackmail."

Not bribery. It wasn't like I was being paid overtime to deal with this mess. Maybe he really had cast a spell on the boss, but she wouldn't be happy to hear me suggest that, and you couldn't cast spells over the phone. The fact that he could easily sabotage our entire business was enough.

"We'll put that theory on hold for now." I absently petted Sky. He stretched out, offering no explanation of what he'd done with those mice. "I wish I could send you to spy on him for me."

"Miaow."

I went to my room and grabbed the bubble wrap. I had a feeling I was going to need some stress relief to get through the rest of this week.

———

The waterfall poured over my head in a shower of glittering water. I shook out my wings, beat them, a thrill racing through my chest as I flew into the air above the lake. My reflection shimmered below. I dropped lower, looking closer. I'd never seen my fairy form up close…

The lake became a mirror. I looked into it and saw a green-skinned thing with bat-like wings and a stranger's face. Huge, luminescent eyes, and teeth as sharp as knives. I recoiled, dread curling through my chest.

Someone stood beside the water. Nathan.

He turned away from the reflection, disgust clear on his face.

Scaly hands reached from the water, grabbed me, and pulled me under.

———

Sky poked me in the cheekbone. Hard. I yelped, feeling blood trickle from the wound. "What is it?"

"Miaow." He purred and rubbed against my face. Maybe he'd known I wanted to wake up.

"Next time just poke me in the leg or something. Not with the claws." I dabbed at my face and looked at my clock. I'd stayed up late reading through my revision notes, and now I'd slept in. I scrambled around looking for my clothes. Despite yesterday's narrow miss, I still hadn't got any actual concrete answers out of Mr Falconer. And now I had to get through yet another day of work, with the clock ticking behind my head.

Three days until my exam. Four until Mr Falconer denied me a wand, unless I figured out who'd cursed his apprentices. No pressure, Blair.

———

Bethan waved the files underneath my face. "Hello? Is there anyone in there?"

"Not really." I yawned and took them. "What's this?"

"Didn't you ask for these?"

"I honestly don't remember." The printer emitted a distinct hissing sound in the background. "That's new."

"We're trialling a new type of ink," Bethan said. "Lizzie is, anyway."

I took the files from her. They glowed all over with colour-changing ink that made me frankly nauseated to look at. "What's the occasion?"

"We're getting a fourth member," said Lizzie. "Veronica wanted us to make welcome posters."

"Yep," said Lizzie. "I'm not saying you haven't done a great job considering how little training you've had, but Blythe did, unfortunately, cover some of our trickiest clients. So we need someone trained in advanced techniques."

"What, like unicorn handling? Compared to Mr Falconer, I could probably do it in my sleep."

"How's the job going, anyway?" Lizzie asked. "I'm guessing not great, given how Veronica keeps griping about how Mr Falconer's out to destroy our reputation?"

"The candidates keep dropping out. I think I've more or less burned through the entire list of grade five wizards and he still won't accept anything less." I exhaled in a sigh. "I'm short on options, to be honest. I was thinking of going for grade fours or just making it up."

Bethan glanced at me from behind her teetering pile of papers. "He won't be happy if he finds out."

"He has me backed into a corner. What does Veronica think?"

She blinked. "What do you mean?"

"Has she spoken to you about him? He seems to have her wrapped around his little finger, which makes no sense considering..." I cut myself off, remembering she wasn't supposed to know all of it. "Considering he's, well, him."

"He's the only—"

"Wand-maker. I know. It's still odd."

"Not exactly. She's always pressuring us to treat problem clients the same as everyone else."

"The guy is more of a recurring catastrophe than a problem client at this point."

Lizzie snickered with laughter from behind a stack of luminous papers. "She's not wrong. I dealt with him last time."

I shook my head. "Yeah, how did you find another grade five? Because there aren't any, not in this town, anyway."

"Graduates," she said. "Look at anyone who's set to graduate this summer. It's only a couple of months away."

Of course. "Good thinking."

"Happy to help. Is he giving you a lot of trouble?"

"You might say that." I put down the neon-inked pages. "Do you know who's most likely to suffer if he stops making wands?"

Lizzie blinked. "The academy, of course. Most witches and wizards have one wand for life."

Hmm. "Has anyone ever lost their wand?"

"Probably," Lizzie said. "Replacing them is expensive. The academy gets a discounted rate. Same with my family's technology."

"What did it used to be like when there were more options? Did people pick and choose who to buy from?"

Lizzie shook her head. "I don't know. It was before I was born."

Bethan looked at me sideways. "Any reason?"

"It's odd that he's the only person left in the entire town who can make wands. I get that there's specialist skills that can't be passed on to just anyone, but if he dies or retires, they lose their only source, right?"

"Theoretically, they can be imported from outside without too much trouble," Bethan said. "But everyone's been using the same wands for years and it'd cause too much disruption to go to another source. Most of us have never known any different."

Hmm. They were too young to remember the other wand-makers and I didn't want to push my luck with

Veronica today. Nor did I want any more innocent apprentices to get caught up in his spell.

Which left me one option: stall him until I figured out how to stop the curse. Of course, the only way to do that would be to send someone in to act as an apprentice in the full knowledge that they risked spending an eternity as a rodent. Admittedly, if he found out my plan, it'd put both of us in the firing line. He was already furious with me.

You'd think the surviving grade five wizards would have formed their own support group by now. Of course, Bethan and Lizzie didn't know the extent of the curse, and exactly what I was asking the potential apprentice to risk.

I looked down at the list of candidates to call today and a name jumped out at me. Leopold —he was a graduate, who'd left university last year. He must have lost his job working as an assistant to Mr Ruther, then. He wasn't really qualified in terms of experience, but he was the only person on the list who came remotely close to matching the criteria.

I slapped a hand to my forehead. If this was a sign from the universe, it wasn't a funny one.

"What is it?" Bethan looked over my shoulder. "You're choosing who to send into the tiger's lair?"

"Essentially," I said. "There's one guy. I don't think he's a grade five wizard, but he fits the bill. He'll probably do what I say, but I reckon I'm storing up some major bad karma for this."

"Yes, you are. It's Mr Falconer. His evilness is rubbing off on you."

"I wouldn't actually send him into the lair alone," I said. "But if I don't start giving Mr Falconer names, he'll start trouncing the company's reputation."

After running through the options in my head, I dialled Leopold's number.

"Hello," I said. "I'm calling about a potential job. Are you interested in working for the wand-maker?"

"Mr Falconer?" he asked, in his slightly high-pitched voice.

"That's him."

"Wait, is this Blair?"

"Yes." I winced inwardly. Leading this innocent guy into a potential trap wasn't fair, especially as I'd once sort of ditched him on a date. No. I just couldn't do it.

"Okay. I'm interested."

"You know he's really grumpy, right?" I said.

"Yes."

"And possibly evil."

"I thought you wanted me to take the job," he said, his brow pinched in confusion. My ability to 'see' a person on the other end of the phone was like a weird one-way video. At least I'd know if I pushed too far.

"I wanted you to know what you're getting into," I told him. "I'm calling you because he's strong-arming me into helping. I know I ditched you before, and I'm sorry for that."

"Eh. You're too old for me anyway."

"Right," I said, having no idea how he expected me to respond to that one. "The job is… look, you're probably best asking me in person, but let's just say nobody has walked away from that position in a year."

"Oh, yeah," he said. "It's cursed, right?"

I nearly dropped the phone. "It's not a good idea to discuss confidential matters this way. But yes."

"Cool. Count me in."

The call ended, leaving me staring at the phone in confusion. "I think I just got called an old maid."

Bethan looked at me. "Old? You?"

"Too old to deal with overconfident guys who think they'll be the exception to Mr Falconer's rule. You know, I'm starting to understand how he managed to dupe so many of them. People aren't willing to believe things until it's too late." Even in the paranormal world, apparently.

Except now I had to explain to Mr Falconer that his new potential apprentice was a few degrees short of qualifying for the position.

9

Mr Falconer, shockingly, did not take the news well.

"Are you joking?" he growled into the phone, as my ability helpfully projected an image of his literally spitting-mad face at me.

"Wizards who aren't at grade five can learn wand-making," I said. "You've taught them before, right? You must have. Otherwise there'd be no grade fives in the town left."

"That isn't good enough," he said. "I will give this apprentice *one* chance, and if he's not good enough, I expect a replacement to be at my office first thing the following morning. No excuses."

And he slammed the phone down.

Poor Leopold. I hoped he knew what he was getting into.

What now?

Answer: do some breaking and entering. I'd failed to teleport into his shop, and it was probably protected against every type of spell. Even the fact that I was doing a job for him might not protect me from his over-extensive security wands, but I was backed into a corner.

Time to see if my potion-making skills were any better than my spellcasting talents.

———

Firstly, I armed myself with a textbook and the leaves I'd gathered when I'd been in the forest. Then I made directly for the classroom at the witches' headquarters. I didn't have a magic lesson tonight since I was supposed to be studying for the exam, so I took the opportunity to pilfer the cauldron and props and take them into an empty classroom.

I'd already triple-checked the ingredient list, but now I read through the recipe twelve times, step by step, muttering them to myself. If I passed the exam, my first potion-making lessons would start next week, so I wasn't *that* far off schedule. Rita had said she'd start with basic recipes with simple steps, few ingredients, and minimal chances for disaster. This particular brew did not count as a simple by any stretch of the imagination, but if I was careful, hopefully I could avoid utter catastrophe.

Ten minutes later, I decided to revise that statement. So far, I'd cut three fingers, wedged a knife into the desk, and now I'd rested my hand on the work surface for all of two seconds and accidentally created an adhesive. On the plus side, the potion was the right colour, simmering away on the stove, but unless I managed to detach my hand from the desk, it'd burn up.

I tugged at my hand, knocking several other ingredients aside in the process. That's what I got for being rash and not telling anyone my plan. I gripped my wrist with my free hand and tugged again, and an empty jar crashed to the floor. At the same time, a familiar voice called from outside, "Is anyone in there?"

Nathan. I called, "Can I have a hand?"

He opened the door and looked at the desk. "It looks like yours is in need of attention."

"Er, yeah, I'm kind of stuck." I wished I'd already bottled some invisibility potion. Sure would come in handy right now.

"Let me see. I'm sure I can unstick you."

He crossed to the sink and poured water onto a cloth. "This should work, unless it's a stickiness potion."

"I wouldn't know how to go about making one of those." I took the cloth in my free hand and rubbed it on my trapped one.

He yanked the knife out of the desk. "What are you making?"

I continued to rub my glue-covered hand. "My first potion. As you can see, it's going swimmingly."

Nathan smiled. "Did you find those mice?"

I shook my head. "Thanks for the other day... sorry my cat decided to derail things."

"Not to worry," he said. "How's the studying going? That's what this is, right?"

"Kind of." *In a few years, it will be, anyway.* "I don't know precisely what the questions on the test will be, so I guess I have to wait and see."

"You're intelligent. You can do this."

Heat burned my cheeks. Since when did he have so much faith in me? "Oh, I forgot to thank you for the bubble wrap," I said, averting my gaze and feeling even stupider for the state my hand was in. "I assume it was you, since the only other person who knows about my weird obsession is Alissa."

He grinned. "You're welcome. I thought you'd appreciate it, considering how stressful your week has been. How's your job going?"

"Not great," I said. "Unless you know what happened to the wand-makers a few decades ago?"

His brow furrowed. "Which wand-makers?"

"It might be nothing," I added. "I got overly curious about why everyone else stopped making wands in the first place, but that probably has nothing to do with whoever's grudge led me into this mess."

"Not necessarily," he said. "It isn't my area of expertise. But it seems like they're putting a disproportionate amount of pressure on you."

"You might say that. I got a lot of use out of the bubble wrap."

He picked up the bottle I'd dropped and put it back on the desk. "That's invisibility. The potion. Right?"

I nearly dropped the damp towel. "How did you know?"

"I'm trained to see through disguises," he said. "Like other tricks paranormals might use to hide."

I'd underestimated him, apparently. "How would you go about seeing through it?"

"It's not easy, but there are always signs. You still leave footprints for a start. You can't quieten your breathing so you don't make any noise. There are spells for that, but everything has its tells."

A paranormal hunter would need to know. But would Mr Falconer?

"Is anyone helping you with this?" he asked.

"I made sure to check the recipe, don't worry." I'd freed three of my fingers, but his presence wasn't doing anything to calm down my nerves, and half my hand was still glued to the desk despite the cloth.

"Have you managed to find anyone for Mr Falconer in the meantime?"

"A desperate graduate who's not technically qualified. I all but told him the truth and he still wants to go ahead with it. So now I have that on my hands, too. Along with the glue. And I annoyed Ava's granddaughter."

"The seer?"

"You've met her?"

"Once or twice. How did you end up annoying her?"

"Ava tried to set up her own wand-making business once and Mr Falconer kicked up a fuss about it. Since the timing of her accident didn't seem coincidental, I wondered if she or her granddaughter might be behind it. But I don't have enough clues."

"So you're making that potion to spy on him?"

Guilty. "It's that or break into Madame Grey's top-secret room and look for information on the history of wand-making to see how he wound up being the only one left, but the curse took effect in the last year, and it probably *is* old Ava. I'm just too curious about how the whole business works." I yanked my hand free and would have knocked a jar over if he hadn't caught my wrist at that moment.

"Careful."

"Ah—thanks." He released my hand, but not before my whole body heated up. Whoa. Since when had mild attraction bloomed into a full-blown crush? I ducked my head and went to wash off the sticky concoction, then returned to the stove. I peered into the cauldron at the simmering potion. "I think it might be done."

"Are you sure?"

I really, really hope so. I gave the concoction one final stir. It was a luminescent green colour, which matched the illustration in the textbook. "I guess I have to drink this. Or tip it over my head, but I'm not really up for that."

Nathan picked up the ingredient list I'd left on the side. "Nothing here is poisonous."

"I know. Trust me, I know what precautions to take." I carefully tipped some of the potion into a beaker, wincing when several drops splashed onto my wrist. "Ah…"

"Did you burn yourself?" he asked, taking a step forward.

"No…" I looked down at my wrist—which had gone see-through. "I'm not sure that's supposed to happen."

His brows shot up. "Look at your arm."

"Oh no." Now my hand was see-through, and my arm had disappeared up to the elbow. And the effect was climbing, fast. "I guess I don't have to drink it, then.

He shook his head. "I can still see you. See through you. The outline of your body is still there."

I looked down at myself. Now most of my chest had vanished and my legs were in danger of going the same way. "I'm supposed to be invisible."

Before my eyes, my body disappeared, inch by inch. Yet the outline remained, like a shadow. I hadn't gone invisible.

I'd gone transparent.

"I was supposed to drink it," I said. "I barely touched it. What in the—?" I broke off, staring at him. "Er. Did you touch it?"

"No." His feet had disappeared. Catching my gaze, he looked down, then up at me again. "I touched you, though."

"Oh no. I think I might have missed a step, or…"

He turned back to the ingredient list. "I'm not the expert here."

I'm not even a novice. "Er, this thing was meant to last for two hours max, but that's if you drink a small amount. And I don't know if there's a counter-spell—"

The half-open classroom door swung open and a teenage girl walked in, staring between Nathan and me in confusion. "Are you supposed to be see-through?"

"No," said Nathan, who'd vanished up to the elbows by this point.

"An accident," I said, my face flaming. Wait, could a transparent person blush?

The girl looked at the cauldron. Sammi was one of

Madame Grey's many grandchildren, Alissa's youngest cousin. "You look like ghosts."

So we did. "It was supposed to be an invisibility potion."

"I think you forgot the nettles," she remarked, eying the green concoction.

"No, I definitely didn't. They were the first—"

Or had I? I turned back to the desk... which had disappeared.

Oh no.

I looked at Nathan. Or through Nathan. Now the desk, the potion and the ingredients had turned transparent, too. "This is ridiculous." I reached for the recipe list and my knee knocked into the desk.

The cauldron tilted.

"Ahh!"

My fingers grasped the cauldron, missed, and wetness drenched my feet as the potion spilt. Nathan caught my hand, and between us, we managed to steady the cauldron before it fell.

Not before the floor had started to vanish, too.

The potion spilt across the floor. Sammi burst into hysterical laughter, at least until it reached her feet. Then she ran.

"Ah!" I hopped up and down on the spot, as cool in a crisis as always. Nathan ran and slammed the door shut, but the potion had already seeped underneath. "We can't stay in here forever. We need the antidote."

"The potion is all over our feet," he pointed out. "We'll spread it everywhere we walk."

I looked through him. Then I burst out laughing. "I'm sorry. I really am. If it's any consolation, there was supposed to be a time limit on it. Two hours."

"Two hours for one dose or the whole cauldron?"

Oh... no. "Do you want me to say I don't know, or the

worst-case scenario? I usually have them memorised just in case."

He shook his head, but looked amused. Or I thought he did, but the transparency made it a little difficult to read his expression. Maybe I hadn't totally blown my chances. "Go on. Tell me the worst."

"Two days," I admitted. "That goes for the entire room, too. And whatever else it touches."

"Ah." He paused as a shriek came from the entrance hall. "I think it got her. I also think you'd better start rehearsing what you're going to tell Madame Grey."

I winced. "I'm dead, aren't I? We need to stop it spreading."

"Doesn't it only work on living things?"

"Nope. Believe me, I wish I'd gone for that variation on the potion, but it's way too complicated. Yes, I know this was, too, but I did just get corrected by a twelve-year-old. And I *nearly* got it right…"

———

'Nearly' wasn't good enough, according to Madame Grey. Upon hearing her granddaughter's shrieks, she'd had the presence of mind to cast some kind of shielding spell on herself and the rest of the building, so it was only the one room and half the entrance hall that had turned see-through. Oh, and her youngest most beloved granddaughter. To say I was in disgrace was an understatement.

On top of that, I was stuck in a transparent state for two days, which she reasoned was punishment enough for my stupidity. I wished Nathan didn't have to be stuck like that, too, though. He'd only been trying to help me.

Finishing her lecture, Madame Grey said, "I can make

what's left of the potion vanish from your shoes, but you're going to have to shower to clean the rest off."

My face heated up again. "Er. I didn't spill the potion on me. Just my shoes. Lucky I didn't drink it either. Why did it affect my whole body?"

"Because it's the way the potion spreads," she said. "It works on anything it touches, and anything that's already covered in the potion can spread it, too. But only within the first minute of touching it. You should be safe to walk home now."

I don't know about safe. I trip over my own feet even when they're fully visible.

"Er..." I hadn't exactly wanted to question her with witnesses, but this was the first time I'd got her alone since Mr Falconer had revealed that something downright odd had happened to the last wand-makers. "I had a question I wanted to ask you. But you weren't around."

Her eyes narrowed. "Did it involve potions that are well beyond your skill level?"

Common sense told me I didn't want to poke her right now. "Is there somewhere I can look up the history of wand-making?"

"Blair, I'd be concerned about ever owning a wand if you're as competent with casting spells as you are with potions."

Ouch. Guess I deserved that one. Still... she definitely kept history books in her office, and it wouldn't be impossible to do some snooping around in my transparent state. On the other hand, going into work would be a disaster, Veronica would ask questions, and my attempts to keep the extent of my investigations from reaching Mr Falconer's ears had thoroughly evaporated. How was I supposed to explain this?

Nathan laughed as I walked into the wall on the way out.

"Oi. I can't see you, but I can hear you." I backed up a step. "I'm not even going to try using these levitating boots in this state."

"You'd think they'd be invisibility proof."

"Ha." I steadied myself against the wall to avoid tripping over my own invisible feet, realised I'd grabbed Nathan instead, and swiftly let go. And then tripped again. "I didn't realise how much I relied on my sight." Maybe it was best that I hadn't achieved full invisibility. "This is hopeless."

"If it's any consolation, you did a spectacular job at your first attempt at a transparency potion. And it's better than the anti-solid potion, which really would turn you into a ghost."

I pinched my own arm. Ow. Definitely still solid. This was going to be fun.

10

I walked into work the following morning, bracing myself for the backlash. I'd debated calling in sick, but after another restless night, I was in dire need of something to take my mind off the chaos I'd unintentionally caused. Madame Grey might even have told Veronica. I didn't get the impression the two of them talked much, but surely word would spread beyond the Meadowsweet Coven. There wasn't any way to hide the fact that I'd accidentally turned half the witches' main headquarters transparent.

On top of that, I'd spilt what was left of the potion, so I didn't even have the necessary ingredients to start from scratch. And there was no way I could risk going into the forest in this state. I hadn't even been able to take advantage of being transparent last night, because it'd taken over an hour for me to walk home, tripping over every other step. Alissa found the whole thing hilarious, Sky was terrified of me, and there was still no sign of the bloody mice.

I'd thought things couldn't get worse, but I was spectacularly wrong. I entered the office—after colliding with the door twice and being unable to find the handle—and an unfamiliar witch looked through me. Her expression creased in confusion.

"Are you a ghost?" she asked uncertainly.

A new co-worker. I really was spectacular at first impressions. The new girl had honey-blond hair and her crisply ironed clothes looked like they belonged on a catwalk. At least nobody would be able to see if I had my shirt on inside out.

"Blair?" said Bethan, staring at me. "Is there something you want to tell us?"

"I may have tried making a complicated potion," I said. "In my defence, it wasn't actually that far off. I'm like this until tomorrow night."

"Seriously?"

"Yep. Long story."

Bethan hid her face behind her files to hide her muffled laughter. "Sorry," she gasped. "That's possibly the most Blair-like thing you've ever done."

"Really glad you find it amusing." I rolled my eyes and turned to the new girl. "Hey, I'm Blair. In two days I'll be back to normal and nobody will ever speak of this again."

Lizzie made a sceptical noise. Bethan snickered. I gave both of them a warning look that probably went unnoticed considering my face was see-through.

"Never," Bethan whispered.

Lizzie nodded, grinning.

The new girl looked utterly perplexed. "Er, hey. I'm Lena," she said, with hints of an Eastern European accent.

"Nice to meet you." I sat down, missing the chair and landing on the floor. Apparently judging where to sit was somewhat more difficult when one's entire body was nearly invisible.

More laughter came from Bethan. The poor new girl looked like she didn't know where to turn.

"This is not a typical day at the office," I said, disentangling myself from Bethan's desk chair and managing to properly sit down this time.

"Yes, it is," said Lizzie. "Weirdness is standard."

"Is that why my files are flashing like traffic lights?" asked Lena, returning to her own desk, which had once been Blythe's.

"New ink," said Lizzie. "It'll wear off in a few hours. Unlike someone's spell."

"Oi." I was glad nobody could see how red my face was. "It was a simple mistake. You can't say you've never seen it before."

"No, I have to say it's a new one," said Bethan. "Anyway, Lena is new in town, like you were a few weeks ago."

"Oh—you lived with normals?" I asked her, momentarily distracted from my ongoing humiliation. Veronica had implied she was more competent at magic than I was, so I'd assumed that meant she'd grown up here.

She nodded. "Yeah, I lived in London for a few years. My dad's side of the family are normals."

"But you aren't? I meant—I'm from a normal town, too. But I was adopted by normals."

I'd been seriously slacking on keeping in touch with them, but I didn't know how much they knew about my real family. Though it was probably for the best that they didn't know that I was about as successful at being a witch as I was at every other job I'd tried.

I went to pick up my files and dropped half of them. Picking up papers one at a time with transparent fingers was torturous enough that Bethan took pity on me and rescued the files, setting them on my desk.

"Are you going to Mr Falconer's place today?" she asked.

"Like this? Definitely not."

"Hmm." Her gaze passed over my transparent form. "That

potion is awfully similar to an invisibility potion. Doesn't have anything to do with the fact that you suspect him of hiding something, right?"

Guilty. I glanced at Lena. It looked like Lizzie was showing her the ropes, so I said, "I can't even pick up the phone, so he's just going to have to live with the disappointment."

"Isn't his new assistant starting today? The one you picked out?"

"Yep." The universe did most definitely not pull its punches. "He doesn't need me to be there, so I'm not going to contact him unless he calls me. I've enough trouble trying to get through this client list when I can't see what I'm doing as it is."

"I can help," she said, "if you tell me how you ended up like that."

"I'm the most inept potion-maker in history."

"I highly doubt it. The academy has incidents all the time. The whole building turned pink once. Did you mean to turn *him* transparent?"

I nearly said it would be an improvement, before remembering that I'd already told her too much. There was little doubt that Mr Falconer was breaking the rules by threatening me *and* Veronica, and the idea that nobody was allowed to or able to intervene infuriated me to no end.

"Okay," I relented. "It was supposed to be an invisibility potion. I followed the recipe to the letter, but one small mistake ended up with this happening. And then I knocked the potion over."

"So that's why our coven meeting has been moved to another location." Her eyes glittered with amusement.

"Probably. Madame Grey wasn't pleased. Her granddaughter got caught in it, too."

She winced. "Oh boy. That's really bad luck."

"You're telling me."

Bad luck, but not impossible to work with. At least I'd turned transparent and not luminescent, and I had a day and a half where most people wouldn't easily be able to spot me. After work, I'd go straight to the man himself and hope he'd left his door unlocked. And that he didn't have killer plants in the garden. Killer *wands,* maybe.

The boss came into the office just as I'd finally figured out how to type with half-visible hands. Veronica's gaze swept the room, from the new assistant to me. She gave a double take. "If you've met an untimely demise, you don't need to come into work."

"I'm not a ghost," I said. "I had an accident making a potion and I'm stuck like this until tomorrow night."

"Interesting."

"Yep." Ah. If anyone would guess the truth, it was her. "I was trying to get ahead on my potion-making skills, except I might have been a bit too ambitious."

"Invisibility."

And now the whole office knew. Wonderful.

"Like I said, an accident."

She frowned at me. "Are you sure you're in a fit state to work?"

"I'm perfectly healthy, just... not quite here. I can pick things up—" I lifted a file, with difficulty. "Kind of. As long as I don't try to use the phone or walk through doors, I can get on with the job."

"Good. Ask Bethan to help." She swept from the office.

Crisis averted. For now. Really, I should have pretended the situation was worse than it actually was and used it as an excuse to go exploring, but doubling my clumsiness would not make me an expert spy. Besides, Mr Falconer would be watching his shop like a hawk—or falcon—during the day. Unless I shadowed his apprentice, but he'd be under close scrutiny, too. No... I was best waiting until dark again.

My phone started to ring. I looked at the number, rolled my eyes, and ignored it. The phone continued to ring. Then Bethan's did, too. Next it would be Veronica. *Why, universe. Why?*

Three attempts to pick up the telephone later and I had it in my hand. "Get over here," Mr Falconer growled.

"That's nice," I said, through gritted teeth, as I fought to keep from dropping the phone. "I'm at work, dealing with other clients."

"I'm your client."

"Can't you tell me what the problem is over the phone?"

"My new assistant," he growled. "I want him gone."

I blinked. "What's the issue with him? Hasn't he only started the job today?"

"He's the worst I've ever had. Won't listen to a word I say, keeps knocking things over..."

I tuned out his ranting as I debated whether to attempt to explain the situation or come up with an excuse. "Sorry, I have another call coming in."

"You—"

I hung up. *Way to take the coward's way out, Blair.* But the man was entirely too sharp. He'd guess my attempt to do some detective work had ended badly. And then? The consequences would land on Veronica and the rest of the company. Not to mention the mice.

The phone rang again.

"Is he allowed to do that?" I asked of nobody in particular. "He's stealing my time from other clients. I should be justified in letting him shout into the void for a bit."

"As Veronica says, he's holding the future of our business in his hands," said Bethan.

"He's just arguing with his new assistant and trying to drag me into it." Poor Leopold.

Veronica opened the door. "The wand-maker is after you."

I groaned. "Sorry. I got him an assistant and he's now calling me to complain about him. I don't know what I'm supposed to do."

"We have to keep our clientele happy."

"I can barely walk through doors without hitting my head in this state," I said. "If I go to see him, I'll probably fall into a ditch."

And now our new co-worker probably thought I was raving mad. I'd thought the same of the others when I'd first come here, but still.

"Speak to him," said Veronica, and left the office.

Bethan gave me a sympathetic glance. "Maybe it won't be too bad. You managed to walk here."

"There was a lot of tripping over my own feet involved." And I hadn't dared switch on my levitating shoes.

Despite his empty threats, Mr Falconer did not call me back, so I took the opportunity to catch up on my teetering list of admin tasks. I should have known the universe would have another surprise in store.

On the way to the coffee machine, Bethan looked out the window. "Huh. That's... weird."

"What is it?" I asked.

"I thought I saw Nathan. But... wait." She swivelled to look at me. "Did he get hit by the spell, too?"

"Yep. Unfortunately. He was on his way to see Madame Grey at the time."

She snickered. "I take it your romantic pursuits are postponed?"

"You're as bad as Alissa. He can't see me, besides."

Bethan swivelled her chair around to face the window.

"He's waving at you. I think. He might just be swatting off a fly."

I groaned. "Are you sure?"

"Yes. Definitely waving at you."

Great. I climbed to my feet, tripped over the desk chair, and walked into the door frame twice trying to get into the reception area.

Callie frowned at me across her desk. "You're creeping me out. You look like a ghost."

"So everyone keeps telling me," I said. "I'm only stuck like this until tomorrow night. Just have to get through the day —" My transparent boot caught on a slightly raised piece of carpet, and I tripped right into Nathan's arms.

"Ah!" I jumped backward into the desk, to the sound of Callie's muffled laughter. "Sorry. Didn't see you walk in."

"No worries," he said. "I came to see how you were getting on."

"We should probably talk outside." I glanced at the boss's office over my shoulder and lowered my voice. "She still seems to think I can effectively do my job like this."

"Watch the door frame," he said, as my shoulder bumped into it. I hadn't noticed it was raining lightly, but if anything, the water made it easier to see him—and me, come to that.

"Sorry, Nathan." I hung my head. "I hope I didn't make it difficult for you to do your job."

"Actually, it's been a lot easier to watch people if they don't know they're being watched. How's it for you?"

"People keep thinking I'm dead. Aside from that, I'm not *that* much more uncoordinated than usual."

"I scared the elves when I went near the forest," Nathan said.

"Wait, the elves?" I asked.

"Yes. They were on the witches' territory again. Not the first incident lately."

"I ran into one of them in the forest, too," I said. "It's where I got the potion ingredients."

His brows rose. "Alone?"

"I was just having a look around. Witches go into the forest all the time. Anyway, I ran into an elf who didn't seem happy about me being there."

He scowled. "Yes, they're certainly pushing boundaries with their territory lately. Typical of their kind."

My stomach fluttered uneasily. Did he think the same of fairies? "Their kind?"

"That particular group of elves has been a nuisance to the witches ever since they moved to the forest."

"Rita told me. She said they kicked up a fuss about the witches being there, but the witches were actually there first. He seemed to really hate Mr Falconer, too. But I know the elves can't have put the curse on him."

"No." He shook his head. "It's not up to me to tell you what to do, but I wouldn't wander into the forest in that state."

"Definitely wasn't on my plan, trust me."

Mr Falconer's place, on the other hand, was fair game... assuming his security wands didn't detect transparent people. Which they might well do. But I was kind of worried for Leopold. If he was as terrible as Mr Falconer seemed to think, it might not even take two or three weeks for him to be fired. Wait, would being fired prevent the curse from coming into effect? *Hmm.*

———

As soon as I got out of the office, I hit the switch on the levitating boots to speed up my pace. Today wasn't as windy, but I still winced every time a current of air threatened to steer me off course on the way to the witches' headquarters.

If I didn't use the boots, it'd have taken me three times as long to walk, so I kept going.

Half the building was still transparent, like a child's drawing that hadn't been fully coloured in. I tiptoed alongside the wall of the non-transparent side, peering through classroom windows to find the one I needed. Madame Grey wasn't in her office—I didn't know what she did during the day, but it involved important head-witchery. I'd just have to utilise the lock-picking skills I'd developed during the phase where I'd flirted with the idea of becoming a cat burglar as an alternate career option.

My own cat would have been appalled at my awkward attempt to climb onto the windowsill. Okay, the window definitely did not unlock from the outside. Inside it was, then.

I entered through the front doors, immediately darting behind the nearest plant pot before I realised nobody was in the entrance hall. Gathering the remaining shreds of my dignity, I walked to Madame Grey's office and tried the lock pick. No luck. She'd probably put a warding spell on the door so the lock couldn't be picked. For all the witchery I'd attempted lately, I was still thinking like a normal.

Think. Alissa had said Rita had the spare key. And *her* classroom wasn't unlocked.

Luck was in my favour for once. Rita wasn't in the classroom. Evening classes didn't start until five, so it wasn't *that* much of a surprise, but I still crept into the room like I was auditioning for *Mission Impossible*. She kept all her keys under the desk, because I'd pilfered the key to the ingredients cabinet during last night's adventure.

I crouched down, feeling for the desk drawer, but it didn't open. She must leave it locked during the day. *Great.*

Wait a moment. The desk wasn't magical. I pulled out my lock pick again, and tried it on the drawer.

Success!

I triumphantly yanked the drawer open, sending keys jangling. There it was. Grabbing the keys, I hurried from the room and ran back to Madame Grey's office before anyone spotted the pair of keys floating past.

I tried several keys before one worked, and exhaled in relief when the office door opened. I had to fully close the door behind me, though I didn't like shutting myself into a room where there wasn't anywhere to hide—transparent or not. A bookcase filled the entire back wall, lined with shelves of ancient books. Pulling them off the shelves and putting them back in the right place would be tricky in this state and would take too much time, especially as Madame Grey knew I'd been trying to make an invisibility potion. She was perceptive enough that she'd work out I'd been snooping if I left a shred of evidence behind, and then I'd be in trouble.

The books were enticing enough, but she also kept the town's records of witchcraft supplies. Wands would be a major feature on the list. I imagined that despite the *one wand per witch or wizard* rule, they'd keep spares in case someone broke or misplaced their wand. I couldn't be the only absent-minded and clumsy witch in the whole town.

I sat in the desk chair and skimmed through the book of records. Aha. The funding for all supplies, wands included, was currently in the hands of the Wormwood Coven, apparently. Not the Meadowsweet Coven, the owners of the town. I'd never heard the name before. It didn't lead anywhere, so I left the book where I'd found it and returned to the shelves. I should have searched a library first, but I'd heard that Madame Grey was in charge of looking after the coven's classified books. The ones detailing the forbidden spells nobody was allowed to use. The mouse curse was illegal, if fairly harmless, but malicious curses were the highest branch of magic and not something you'd find in a regular textbook.

Forbidden curses. There it was. I slid the book from the shelf and opened it to the introductory page, the old cover catching on my clumsy hands.

The first line leapt out at me: all curses were invented. While some spells were universal, curses were specific and depended on the individual's magical prowess. *To cast a curse requires considerable skill and intent.*

Nothing new there…

To cast a curse towards an object or person, one must direct the curse at the person in question, or be in close proximity. If the intended target isn't present or has a powerful magical defence present, then the curse will rebound on its owner or anyone else unlucky enough to be nearby. Even an unintentional victim is enough to guarantee one's arrest if the effects of the curse are severe…

So all curses found a target even if they weren't intended that way at all. For a wand-maker, it wasn't outside the realm of possibility that he'd made himself immune to curses and left someone else to take the fall. But he'd said he didn't recall anyone actually casting the curse on him. Ava's granddaughter had flat-out said she hadn't done it, unless she'd slipped it into their argument. But then, she wouldn't have been able to lie to me without my knowing.

I returned the book to the shelf, doing my best to keep that relevant information in my head. I didn't have long before the other witches and wizards came in for their lessons and I needed to lock the office and put Rita's keys back where they belonged before someone else showed up. Besides, it wouldn't stay light outside forever, and there were a number of places that might be more likely to give me specific information relating to the curse. I didn't need to be transparent to speak to Ava, but maybe Annabel had hidden something at the cottage. There was also Mr Falconer's place, but he'd be on the lookout for trouble, and I'd pushed my luck far enough today already. Let's face it, as long as he had those sentinel wands on duty, sneaking inside would be a distant prospect. But if Leopold had survived his first day, he'd be staying in the shop himself, and might be able to tell me something useful.

I crept across the office and carefully locked the door behind me before heading into Rita's classroom to return the keys to her desk.

Then I left the witches' headquarters, switched on the levitating boots, and made my way to Ava's granddaughter's house. Unlike Mr Falconer's shop, her house wasn't warded, and she had only the one wand to defend herself with. I wasn't looking for a confrontation, but maybe she'd see reason if I told her innocent lives were at stake.

It'd started to rain again when I'd been in the witches' place. Raindrops dripped off my transparent hands and probably the rest of my body, too. Hmm. Maybe this wasn't a good idea. Anyone who looked at me would see a half-drowned ghost.

I switched the boots off at the end of the road, seeing a female figure walking down the path into the forest. Why was Annabel going into the woods in the rain? I turned the boots back on and followed slowly, counting on the trees to hide my presence.

Then I stopped. Annabel stood face to face with an elf—not the one I'd spoken to, but another one. They conversed in whispers, occasionally glancing around, but I'd concealed myself behind a tree. I didn't hear all the words, but I got the gist. Were relationships between witches and elves allowed? I hadn't heard otherwise, but given their history, no wonder she'd sneaked into the woods out of sight of the other witches' houses.

Watching someone else's private conversation made me distinctly uncomfortable, so I backed slowly away, memorising the elf's features so I'd recognise him if I ran into him later.

As Annabel turned away to head back home, I swiftly floated back down the path, out of sight of both of them. I could replace my ingredient supplies, but they'd be visible for all to see when I put them in my pocket, and I doubted I'd be allowed unsupervised use of the cauldron for long enough to brew up Invisibility Round Two. *And I don't have long until the exam.* Until my fate would be sealed and, if I didn't play my cards right, I'd be left wandless.

Mr Falconer was in, judging by the light in the single window. Since Annabel had returned home, I hadn't been able to sneak into her house, and let's face it, I wouldn't be sneaking anywhere as long as I kept dripping rainwater wherever I went.

I floated upwards to look through the windows, figuring it'd got dark enough for me not to be spotted. I was sure the answers were inside. If I hadn't failed so badly at my potion-making attempt, I'd have considered using another one to get him to admit the truth himself, but he was doubtless wise to that kind of trick. The only witnesses were—

Mice.

I dropped to the ground, sure I'd seen a tail disappear under the hedge. *Yes. There it is.*

"So you *did* come back here?" I crouched down. "What is it?"

They probably couldn't even see me. The mice kept running, and I followed, floating down the road—

I nearly fell out of the air.

At the end of the road, there was a body.

I screamed. And kept screaming. There'd be rumours of a

screaming ghost for the next week, but never mind that. Mr Falconer was *dead.*

My feet touched the ground as I backed away and ran to the shop. Leopold might be around, assuming he hadn't been fired—but the door was locked. I grabbed and pulled at the handle, but it wouldn't budge.

"Blair?" said Nathan's voice out of thin air beside me.

"Get the police." My voice shook. "Mr Falconer is dead. Someone killed him."

He couldn't be dead. He just couldn't. I backed away from the door, and abruptly discovered that vomiting transparently did not make it less messy.

Nathan walked towards the body as I pointed without looking in that direction. There was a long pause, then he returned to the shop entrance. "Yes, he's dead. Someone snapped his neck. Looks like a spell. I wouldn't let them find you here."

"They can't seriously blame me? I don't even have a wand."

My mind spun. He'd been an awful person, but he was also the only wand-maker and the last week had hammered home how dependent the town was on him. Even those who hated him.

Who could have done this? The elves? Or—Ava? Surely not. Besides, she was under twenty-four-hour watch and didn't even have a proper wand. And I'd *seen* Annabel, so she had a rock-solid alibi. Of course, it was entirely possible someone had decided to kill him now for some other reason than the curse. But my suspicions refused to be buried. After all, I'd come so close to solving the mystery. I'd been almost certain he was partially responsible himself, and now he was gone. Taking any chance I had at catching the person who'd cursed the assistants along with him.

11

The atmosphere at work the next day was subdued to say the least. The problem client—or recurring catastrophe—was finally out of our hair, but he'd left such a void behind that I found myself completely unable to concentrate.

Part of that was because I was still transparent, but this time nobody laughed when I fell out of my seat, dropped the phone or scattered my files. I'd barely slept, and what little sleep I'd managed to get was plagued with nightmares. Not even about Mr Falconer, but about waking up and still being transparent—except actually being a literal ghost this time. On top of that, the mice were still missing, and my exam was tomorrow. Reading over my revision notes was like tipping water through a sieve. If I'd retained any information at all from Rita's lessons, I really hoped it resurfaced when I sat the exam, otherwise I might as well send the cat in my place.

I'd thought things couldn't possibly get any worse, but I should have known better than to challenge the universe at this point.

"Your phone's ringing, Blair," said Bethan, moving a stack of files aside.

I frowned in puzzlement. "It's not—" Oh. She meant my mobile phone, which I kept in my handbag. I fished it out and saw Alissa was calling me. She never called me at work, since we were both usually run off our feet.

It took me two attempts to hit the answer button. "Alissa?"

"Ava's granddaughter has been arrested."

My heart lurched. "No."

"It's true. She's—distraught." Alissa sounded it, too. "It's been hard to deal with. They're rounding up suspects left and right. The man might have been awful, but killing the only wand-maker…"

I'd been too out of it last night and this morning to ask how the rest of the town had reacted, but I'd assumed the people I'd been questioning would be safe from arrest unless they'd done something to implicate themselves. After all, as far as the police knew, Nathan had discovered the body himself. He'd covered for me, so Steve didn't have me arrested for being near the murder scene. I didn't even have words to express my gratitude, and yet Annabel was the one person who'd had an alibi.

"Does Steve the Gargoyle believe she did it?" I asked.

"No idea. I'm just passing on what I heard. She got arrested, and there are other names on his list, too."

"Oh no. What about his apprentice?"

"Wait—you found someone? Before he died?"

"I swear I told you." The last few days had been so confusing. "Leopold. Mr Falconer was never going to keep him around, but I haven't seen him since. I guess he was staying in the shop, but—" *The door was locked,* I wanted to say, but the others in the office didn't know I'd been there. Only Alissa and Nathan did.

"Sorry, I haven't heard a word about Leopold. Everyone's talking about Falconer, though. Why did he not defend himself?"

"He didn't?" I hadn't looked close enough to determine the cause of death, since the little I'd seen had given me enough nightmares.

Alissa exhaled. "Apparently not, according to the reports from the crime scene."

That can't be right. Those wands of his threw tantrums and spat out sparks when he was angry. How was this possible?

Bethan leaned over and whispered, "The boss is coming."

"I have to go," I said, and hung up.

I hadn't come to any conclusions about how, exactly, he'd died. That wasn't my job. But the man had a few thousand wands inside his shop, and he'd been down the road from his own front door when he'd died. How could anyone have got close enough to murder him?

The office door flew inward and Veronica sailed in, wearing a periwinkle-blue suit. "This is quite a dilemma."

That was one way of putting it.

There were a few murmurs of agreement from the others.

"Our client is dead." She spoke matter-of-factly, but it was like hearing a quiet declaration from a thunderstorm. Not threatening. Still terrifying. "That will pose problems for us."

"Why?" asked Bethan. "Clearly it has nothing to do with us. We found him an assistant, same as usual."

"Precisely."

"Wait, do people think Leopold did it?" I asked. "He can't have. He was harmless." *And not even qualified, I* added silently. "Of all people, he's the least likely. He was desperate for a job, and he wouldn't have killed off his employer."

"I suppose not," she said. "I've been called to a meeting of the covens while we discuss what to do about the craft of wand-making."

"You have?" I asked. "The other wand-makers stopped making any wands decades ago, right? Is there anyone else who can take over for him?" Probably not, if they really had all lost their memories fifty years ago.

"That's what we're meeting to decide," she said. "As for you… I'd suggest you all go home, and recuperate. Especially you, Blair." Her gaze lingered on me for a moment and I held my breath, certain she suspected I was involved. But she left without saying another word.

I wanted nothing more than to go home and bury myself under my bedcovers, but I had less than a day of being almost invisible left, and several potentially innocent people to save. Mr Falconer's death had completely thrown me off. What would happen to the mice now? Would they stay stuck forever, or would the curse wear off, with its target dead?

Either way, maybe the security on his shop wouldn't be as stringent now he was gone. Some spells needed the caster to be alive to work, though I was far from an expert on the subject. But maybe the mice could be turned back without having to undo the curse.

Or maybe they'd seen who'd killed him. I doubted the gargoyles would have thought to question a bunch of rodents, unless Nathan had told them.

I walked to Mr Falconer's shop, relieved it wasn't raining this time, though mud still streaked the road and made it impossible to hide my footsteps. I approached the door and found my way barred by a strange shimmering line of material, wrapped around the entire shop. Paranormal police tape? *This was a bad idea.* The mice must still be inside, alone. Someone needed to tell the police they were human.

A hand rested on my transparent shoulder, and Steve the Gargoyle loomed over me. "I knew I'd catch a rat. Or mouse."

"Don't kill the mice!" I said, alarmed. "Please don't."

"That's an odd request for someone who's about to get

arrested."

What? "No. I'm not the killer. I wouldn't be returning to the murder scene if I was."

He didn't let go. "I'm aware you're not a ghost, Miss Wilkes, but there are some disturbing stories about you going around. You're coming with me."

———

I sat transparently in my cell, my legs aching from the discomfort of the wooden bench, eyes squinting against the darkness. There were lanterns in the corridor, like an old-fashioned dungeon, but nothing within the cell itself, and my imagination kept itself busy conjuring up images of things that might be hiding in the corners.

When Steve had brought me to the police station, I hadn't thought he'd really lock me up without letting me say my piece, but he'd ignored my protests and handed me over to another gargoyle the moment we'd arrived at the jail next to the police station. That gargoyle had led me down a corridor into the dark, and here I was.

I hated dark, cold places. My skin crawled all over, and looking through my own transparent feet made the place even more creepy. Unfortunately, nobody had bothered to ask any questions before throwing me in here. Not even how I'd ended up transparent. If only I'd managed to get that spell right… well, maybe I still wouldn't have any answers, but at least I wouldn't be stuck in this horrible cell. It smelled like something had decomposed in here… several times over. I gave up holding my breath because it made me dizzy, and just resigned myself to smelling of this place for a week after I got out.

If I got out.

You're innocent. They can't keep you here forever. Not even the notoriously harsh paranormal police. Right?

I had no idea what human police stations looked like, but the paranormal prison was dark and dank, like a dungeon aboveground that hadn't been cleaned in a few decades. Mould on the walls and floor. Cockroaches in the corner. Maybe I'd be expected to eat them. Not that I was particularly hungry, though I'd been sitting here for hours.

After some indeterminate amount of time, I looked up at the click of a lock as someone unlocked the cell. A gargoyle I didn't know beckoned me to come out. Like the chief of police, he was a huge brute of a man even in his human form. My sixth sense showed me images of fists like rocks, cruel smiles and wings, and then leapt into overdrive when I left the cell itself. Images of the other prisoners' paranormal types bombarded me all the way down the corridor, from witches and wizards to goblins and shifters. They watched with fascination as I transparently walked past, tripping over in the dim light several times. The gargoyle glared at me like I was doing it on purpose. I wished I *had* pretended to be dead. Ghosts couldn't get arrested. But as accomplished as I was at pretending, I should probably draw the line at faking my own death.

The interrogation chamber was a bright cold room with stone walls. My interrogators were all gargoyles. Four large muscular men with very serious faces, looking at me as though my transparent state was a personal insult.

"I didn't kill Mr Falconer," I said, for the fourth time. "I was at his shop because I was looking for his apprentice."

Considering how much I'd had to fudge my story to cover up that I'd been spying on him, I was glad to be the only person in the room with an inner lie detector.

Steve the Gargoyle, the biggest, most stony-faced of the lot of them, glared at me. "Most murderers aren't stupid enough to return to the scene of the crime."

"I'm not the murderer," I said. My head throbbed painfully, the bright lights a sharp contrast to the dark cell. "I told you, I was looking for his new assistant. I worried he might have been hurt, too."

"Which assistant?"

"Leopold. He just started working for Mr Falconer, since I helped him find a job," I explained. "I hadn't heard an update so I went to check he hadn't been hurt."

"The assistant quit his position that morning. We've already questioned him and found he had an alibi. Seems he was at the Laughing Pixie while the murder took place. But nobody can verify where *you* were."

"I was on my way to check on him. I was supposed to go there to see how he was getting on, but…" I gestured at my transparent body. "I had an accident while making potions and wasn't able to. But Mr Falconer was pretty insistent that Leopold wasn't the man for the job and that I'd need to find him a replacement, immediately."

"And for that, you killed him?"

"No, I told you I didn't." It was like talking to, well, a piece of stone. "I didn't know Mr Falconer was going to turn up dead. But I can help."

"No," Steve said flatly.

One of the other gargoyles cut in. "She did bring us to Mr Bayer's killer."

Steve snorted. "Pure luck. She's not even a proper witch."

Maybe he wasn't wrong, but that wasn't his call to make. I wondered if Madame Grey had heard about my arrest yet. "Whatever I am is irrelevant. Except not guilty. Which I'm not."

"Nobody could see you, could they?" Steve said. "That's convenient."

"You can all see me," I pointed out. "Who else have you arrested?"

"That," he said, "is none of your business. It seems to me that you killed him, and then made yourself invisible to cover up the crime?"

"Er, excuse me?" I spluttered. "This was an accident, and I'm transparent, not invisible. It happened two days ago." The potion also should have worn off by now, which was worrying. Maybe permanent transparency would work in my favour if I was doomed to be jailed for life for a crime I hadn't committed.

Steve tutted. "Conveniently, we wouldn't be able to see bloodstains on you in that state."

I resisted the impulse to sigh. "I didn't do it."

"You said he was a problem client."

"There are a lot of problem clients. I was supposed to be getting a wand from him this weekend. I wouldn't kill the only wand-maker in town. Wouldn't kill anyone, in fact. As I said." My head really hurt, and I kind of felt like I might vomit all over his feet.

"Your track record does you no favours," he said. "You've broken enough of our rules."

"What?" I said, genuinely shocked. "I've never broken any paranormal laws. It's not illegal that I went to his place yesterday, either. I never thought anyone would kill him. He was going to sell me a wand. I wanted one more than anything. Ask Madame Grey."

I'd said the magic word. His expression stilled, and he turned to the others. "We'll make a decision on your case by tomorrow morning," he said. "For now, you'll return to your cell."

"But—" I protested. "I have an important exam tomorrow."

I'd long since given up hope of getting any closer to the person responsible for the curse, but the potion would surely wear off soon, along with my chance of doing any more snooping without being caught. I should be relieved to have the burden taken off my hands, and yet I still hadn't actually managed to do anything useful. But how was I supposed to know someone—maybe the person responsible for the curse —would kill the man I was helping before I had the chance to get any results? I'd assumed they'd cursed the job because they didn't want to kill the only wand-maker. I was wrong. At least, if it was the same person.

If the killer had struck because I was close to the truth, I'd partially caused his murder. I had to solve it.

———

Cold. Damp. My wings beat, but I was trapped... trapped in a confined space...

I jerked upright, blinking into the darkness as my door clicked open. I couldn't have slept for long, because I was still transparent.

Someone came into the room. The outline of someone I couldn't see. Either Nathan or an actual, genuine ghost. My heart rate kicked into gear.

"Please tell me I got the right cell," Nathan's voice said from somewhere to my right.

I jumped upright in relief. "Yes, you did. Are you breaking me out of jail?"

"No. I managed to convince Steve that there wasn't enough evidence to hold you in here indefinitely. We should leave before he changes his mind."

"I find it hard to believe anyone could convince Steve, to be honest. He has it in for me, even though with Mr Bayer, I *caught* the killer." I stumbled on the way out the door and knocked into him sideways. "Ow. Sorry."

"It was somewhat difficult to find you like this."

I could imagine. There were no lights in here. I had to

lean on Nathan at one point on the way out, and I couldn't even appreciate the moment.

"I'll walk you home," he said, when we emerged from the jail, into the darkness. It must be the middle of the night by now. "I thought the potion was supposed to wear off tonight?"

"It is," I said. "Sorry. I made a real mess of things."

"You aren't responsible," he said, his voice gentle. "Steve shouldn't have reacted the way he did."

I shook my head, though he probably didn't see it. "I was snooping around and got caught. It's my own fault. I just wanted to see where the mice went. They might have seen who did it."

"I can look for them," he said. "I have permission to be near the crime scene. I think you did me a favour by turning me transparent, Blair. Otherwise I might have been the one on security duty when he was killed."

I swallowed hard. Thinking about Nathan being hurt made me want to burst into hysterical tears.

He let me lean on him on the walk back, probably more to stop me falling into the mud than for comfort's sake, but I appreciated it. When we reached the house, he paused.

"I hope you don't blame yourself for this, Blair," he said, his voice soft.

"I feel at least partly responsible," I said. "I don't know who might have done it. Maybe someone who was afraid I was close to solving the case—but the evidence all suggested he brought the curse on himself. Killing him wouldn't achieve anything."

"Brought it on himself?" he echoed.

I shook my head. "Never mind. It's pretty much irrelevant now he's dead. I think the person who put the curse on him was aiming at him and got his assistants instead. I hope they're not stuck like that forever now."

"They won't be," he said. "If he was the target, the curse should have been broken when he died. Steve sent the other gargoyles to search the area nearby after finding the body. He didn't mention any mice."

Wait. If the assistants were still stuck in rodent form, then maybe I'd been wrong all along and Mr Falconer hadn't been the intended target of the curse. Snooping around his shop right now was out of the question, but I wished I knew for certain if the assistants had escaped or not.

I really hope so.

I tripped over the threshold to the house and rapped on the flat door, too tired to find my keys.

Alissa appeared a moment later. "Blair! I thought you were going to be stuck there overnight."

"Got lucky." I tripped past her into the flat, and collapsed onto the sofa. Sky wriggled out from underneath me with an indignant yowl. "Nice to see you, too."

"He's been howling all night," Alissa said.

"No mice?"

"No mice. He seemed pretty distraught. I told you he was your familiar."

"I can't—I don't think I'm ever getting a wand now." I crawled into an upright position as Alissa leaned over and hugged me.

"It's unjust, what happened to you. They shouldn't have blamed you."

I exhaled heavily. "I walked into a crime scene when I knew Steve the Gargoyle had it in for me. And I completely failed to save those apprentices *or* find out what Mr Falconer was hiding."

"Don't be so hard on yourself," said Alissa. "You did your best."

"I was so sure Mr Falconer put the curse on the job himself to keep his secrets, or Ava was responsible. Maybe a bit of both. I mean, he annoyed so many people. Anyone might have killed him. There's not even any proof that it's connected to my investigation."

"He died right as you were getting close to the answers," she said. "I'd say that's proof enough."

"Not for Steve the Stony-Faced Gargoyle."

She snorted. "Sorry, this isn't funny in the slightest."

I managed a smile. "I've gone from dealing with a bad-tempered wand-maker to a grumpy gargoyle. Not much of an improvement."

"You don't have to deal with him now you're free," she said. "Nobody will expect you to find Mr Falconer's replacement. The witches are still discussing it."

"I wouldn't have thought there'd be no backup plan. Even with all the apprentices turning into mice, surely someone would have noticed that there wasn't anyone else who had the same training."

"Oh, I don't doubt Madame Grey will have come up with something. We just have to wait to find out."

And hope the new person didn't meet the same fate.

"Oh yeah," she said. "Madame Grey told me that your exam's been postponed until Saturday, in light of your arrest. She sent Nathan to set you free."

"She did?" So he hadn't come to rescue me of his own accord. I didn't even have the energy to be mildly disappointed. At least I'd get another shot at the exam, if I pulled myself together.

I rubbed a hand over my forehead. A hand I could suddenly see.

Alissa's eyes widened. "Hey! The potion wore off."

"Yay." I mimed a celebratory dance. "I can't get out of work tomorrow, then. Heaven knows what the boss will have to say."

12

"I'm glad it was him," was the first thing the boss said the following morning.

Bethan spat out a mouthful of coffee. "Excuse me?"

Veronica said. "Of all the clients to lose, I liked him the least."

Why did you have to push me to help him? I shut down the thought before I accidentally said it aloud. I'd hardly slept, and not being transparent only caused my total mess of an appearance to be more obvious to everyone. I'd kind of hoped the boss would take pity on me and reduce my workload, but the looming pile of everything I'd not dealt with this week rivalled Bethan's overly messy desk.

"That's not a polite thing to say about a dead person," Bethan said.

"Especially the only wand-maker," I added. "Have you—and Madame Grey—come up with a contingency plan yet?"

"No," she said, tersely. "The idiotic man has locked up his shop so nobody can get into it."

"But—" I cut off as she left the office. "But that means nobody can get at the wands."

So much for at least getting a wand out of this mess.

"I'm sure Madame Grey will think of something," Bethan said consolingly.

"Did the boss really just say that?" said Lena, who looked on the brink of handing in her notice. "Do clients normally die on the job?"

There was an awkward pause in which the other two did their best not to look at me, and I did my best to look… nowhere. "Nope," Lizzie said. "I have good news, though—I fixed the printer."

The printer made a coughing noise and spat a wad of paper at Bethan. She looked down at it. "It's purple."

"It's an improvement," Lizzie insisted.

I looked down at my own paper. My headache had subsided for now, courtesy of a mug of motivational coffee, but the looming spectre of Mr Falconer's death hung heavily over all of us.

One advantage to his death: I wasn't the only person prying into his history to see who might have been the one to bump him off. The murderer plainly hadn't thought too hard about that. Or hadn't cared. Throughout the day, theories flew wildly around the office whenever anyone got a spare moment—outlandish tales of illicit affairs and secret relationships, even a love child or two.

"It's because they haven't found a will yet," said Bethan. "Nobody knows who will get his wand collection. Common sense says they'll donate it to the academy, or maybe just have someone else in charge of the shop so people can order their wands same as usual. There's enough supplies for a while, at least."

"When they figure out how to get in," I pointed out.

"What if someone isn't compatible with *any* of the wands at all?"

She shook her head. "No clue. I don't know how they're going to divide up the rest of his possessions, considering he had no family."

"No apprentice either," added Lizzie. "That's not our job, thankfully. Veronica might be insensitive, but at least she removed us from the case. None of us is qualified to find an actual wand-maker."

Nope. Definitely not. But with the academy set to inherit his entire wand collection, it was time to talk to Helen again.

———

Since the big event was tomorrow, I expected to find Helen in the park setting up the finishing touches on the stage, and I wasn't disappointed.

"Blair!" She waved at me from behind a row of chairs she'd been levitating. "Changed your mind after all?"

"Er, sorry. My exam's been moved to tomorrow instead. And I've had… a week." I probably looked as bad as I sounded.

"I heard," she said, sympathy spreading across her face. "I knew you were innocent and they wouldn't keep you locked up for long."

"Like I said, I was doing a job for Mr Falconer," I said. "I don't understand why anyone would kill him. He was the only wand-maker."

She nodded, lowering the chairs with a flick of her wand. "It's a bad situation all around. I'm not yet sure how we're going to handle things at the academy, but we should have enough wands to last us through the next year, at least."

"I thought you were set to inherit the lot," I said to her. "I'll be getting one if I pass the exam, but nobody can get into the shop. That's why I wondered. But I'm curious… he really wasn't well-liked. Do you have an idea about who might have done it?"

She shook her head. "Why, are you investigating again? There's a dozen people who might have buried him in a coffin, given the chance. He's—he was—possibly the least popular of our residents."

"I didn't know there was a list."

She lowered her wand. "Not a list… no, that was a joke, right?" Her smile came back, but it looked false. "It's just, you know, he's lived here long enough to have met generations of witches and wizards."

"Yeah, that's why I'm surprised he never trained anyone else," I said. "Unless… there used to be other wand-makers, right?"

The Wormwood Coven. What with the upheaval of his death, I hadn't thought to ask anyone about the coven who supposedly funded the town's wand supplies. But asking anyone that might involve giving away that I'd broken into Madame Grey's office.

"Before I was born," Helen responded. "I'm sorry. I wish there was something I could do."

Sincerity permeated her words. Helen didn't know any more than I did, and I should really stop poking further. I ought to be celebrating not being transparent, not mourning the death of a man who'd driven me out of my mind for a week. Well, not mourning him, but his victims. Reportedly, Ava's granddaughter remained jailed, and knowing Steve was looking for an excuse to lock me up again, I didn't dare plead her case.

No… the person to talk to was someone I should have asked from the start: Madame Grey.

I hadn't seen or spoken to Madame Grey since my accidental transparency, but by now, the spell would have worn off Sammi. I guessed the same was true for Nathan, but I didn't know where he spent his days. Possibly, he was still dealing with Steve the Gargoyle. I wasn't at all keen for another chat with the chief of police, so I made for the witches' headquarters instead.

The good news: the place was no longer transparent. The bad news: the moment I walked inside, I nearly collided with Madame Grey herself.

The leading witch gave me a stern look. "Blair. Good to see you're more substantial this time."

"Is Sammi okay?"

"If you mean to ask if the spell wore off, it did. You actually did a good job with that particular potion, if it wasn't what you planned to make. I have a feeling you're going to need training in moderation."

I hesitated. "Er... will I be able to get a wand? I heard nobody can get into the shop."

"The coven keeps their own supply," she said. "I think we'll be able to deal with it."

Not the reaction I'd expected. "I thought he was the only wand-maker, and the academy was inheriting all the wands."

"Who told you that?"

"There were a bunch of rumours flying around at work," I said vaguely. She didn't know about my transparent tryst into her office, and I had no intention of enlightening her on the subject. "But—I was working for him, when he died, and I feel like they've locked up the wrong people."

"What makes you think that?"

I paused before saying, "He told me not to tell anyone, but I guess it doesn't matter now he's dead. His apprentices keep falling under a spell. A curse. I was close to figuring out who did it when he died."

Her brows rose. "Where are these apprentices?"

I told her the short version of the story. "They were all turned into mice. He had a cage in his shop, but obviously I haven't been in the place since before he died, and it's locked. I don't know if they're still there. I'm not sure what he was doing when they killed him—or who did it. But the mice might know." I'd never, in my previous life, thought I'd be saying *that* with a straight face.

Madame Grey began to walk in the direction of her office. "I assumed there was an issue with his apprentices, but he decided against telling the covens."

"Yeah, he really didn't want me to tell you," I said. "What I don't understand is what someone would have to gain from this. Killing the only wand-maker. What's the backup plan? The academy—a friend I have who works there, she seems to think that it'll work out and someone else will take over. But I thought everyone else quit."

"How did you know that?"

"Vincent told me," I said. "The elder vampire. He said he didn't remember it well, but that the former coven who used to make wands had some kind of an accident that caused them to lose their memories."

"He would be correct," she said. "But it was no accident. The coven decided to erase their memories of the craft on purpose, or so we believe. In any case, one day they knew, and the next, they didn't."

My jaw hung loose. "They did it deliberately? And Mr Falconer was the only one left?"

"Not at the time. The others died off, gradually, until only he remained. Unfortunately, the others had not spread the knowledge beyond their own covens, which leaves us with our present dilemma."

My heart dropped. "You don't have a replacement. Right?"

"As of the present moment—no. If I were you, Blair, I'd

concentrate on studying for your exam tomorrow. Leave the investigation to the police."

"But—Ava. Her granddaughter's been arrested. She's innocent. I—"

"Blair, you have a good heart. Your mother was the same."

My heart seized. Did she have to bring up my family? I'd tried so hard, and yet everywhere I looked, chaos seemed to erupt. And I'd hoped so hard that I'd be heading to Mr Falconer's shop this weekend to pick out my wand after beating the curse.

Speaking of wands… Madame Grey's was in her upper pocket, where she usually kept it. I couldn't help noticing it was branded silver. Like the one in the window display.

"Your wand," I said. "It's different to the others. I mean, to the ones in his shop."

She frowned. "Naturally. He wasn't a wand-maker when I was younger."

The wand had been made before he'd taken over the business. So another wand-maker must have been responsible.

"Are there big differences between the newer wands and the older ones?" I asked. "I imagine the safety constraints are stricter, like the broomsticks."

"You aren't wrong. You can do all sorts of things with an older wand that it's not possible to do with the newer models," she said. "There's a reason you can't cast spells through solid objects, or put a spell *on* someone's wand. It used to be possible to do that, but the number of accidents was appalling, so that rule was brought in quite some time ago."

"How many of the rules were Mr Falconer responsible for?" I didn't picture him being particularly concerned with safety.

"None of them. It was up to the covens. But I'd advise you to forget about the man, and the curse. It's sad that you were so closely involved with him before his death, but if there is a curse, then doubtless his death will have taken care of it."

I frowned. "So they'll definitely be human again?"

"If the curse was cast on him, then yes. They'll have turned human again."

But they didn't. Otherwise, surely one of them would have shown up by now, and told the police who the killer was. Right?

"One thing, Blair," said Madame Grey. "I have to ask—what were you doing at the crime scene?"

"Looking for the mice," I said. "Some of them were at my flat, but they ran away. Alissa's cat kept chasing them, but mine… I think he knew they were human."

Her eyebrows disappeared into her hairline. "Cat?" she echoed. "Is this the familiar Alissa mentioned? We're going to have to look into that situation after you get a wand."

"Er. *If* I get a wand."

"We're going ahead as planned," she said. "If you've studied for your test, you'll have no trouble."

Studied. Right. Between snooping around and being arrested.

"Also," she added, "when I spoke to the police, I told them not to keep you in custody and that your presence at the crime scene was likely an accident. I won't be able to do the same thing again."

"Oh," I said. "Thank you." Well, that was me put in my place. What in the world was I supposed to do now?

I could always go to Annabel's house and look for more clues, but the police would probably be watching the place. Same with Ava at the hospital. But if the curse really had been aimed at the apprentices, I doubted either of them would have been responsible.

I'd been so certain Mr Falconer had a nefarious secret that explained how he'd ended up being the only wand-maker. His death, however, had completely unravelled all my theories and created a thousand new ones, not least about who might take his place. The only people who'd undertaken the bare minimum of wand-making training were currently running around as mice, and possibly being eaten by wildlife. Unless they'd turned back…

I walked to Oswald's mother's house, hoping that she wouldn't think I was unhinged, and rang the doorbell.

"I'm sorry to disturb you," I said. "I wondered—has your son come home?"

"No," she said. "Why—is he in trouble? Has something changed?"

I shook my head. "Nothing. Sorry to disturb you."

No lies. The mice hadn't turned human. The curse had been aimed at them—but the only way to know for sure was to catch one of them.

———

I found Sky lounging in the doorway when I got home, apparently with the intention of tripping me up.

"Sky." I stopped walking, letting the door swing shut behind me. "I need your help. Can you bring me one of the mice?"

He blinked his grey-and-blue eyes, and went back to washing himself.

"Don't pretend not to understand me. I know you do. You brought the mice here once. Why'd you chase them off in the first place?"

"Miaow."

I crouched next to him. "Please? You know this is important. The mice must know who killed Mr Falconer. They might even know who set off the curse, so I can undo it. Can't you find just one of them?"

Sky miaowed again and licked a paw, unmoving. I stepped over him to get into the flat. If this was an example of what familiar training might be like, I might as well take one of the mice as a familiar.

"Sorry," said Alissa, when I'd updated her on the latest. "Maybe the mice weren't what we thought."

I shook my head. "They're still out there, and haven't gone back to their families yet. I think that means the curse is still active. Is there a spell to make animals talk?"

Her eyes rounded with understanding. "There is. I think I might have to look that one up... I'm not sure it works on animals that weren't animals to begin with, though."

"Then maybe a spell that makes me able to understand animal speech?" I suggested. "Yes, I know the possible ways *that* could go wrong. But first I need to actually find one of the mice, otherwise I'd be wasting my time."

She nodded slowly. "That's a great idea. It's not a difficult spell—most of us have used it on our familiars at one time or another just to see what would happen."

"Wait, you've used it on Roald before?"

She nodded. "Yeah. He didn't care for it much. All he wanted to talk about was food."

I grinned. "I think Sky would probably be the same. He's an enigma. I was so sure those mice were the real deal. Typical."

"Let's not give up just yet," she said. "Not all of them will have been in the shop, right?"

"No," I said. "Actually, my plan was to go to the police station first. Annabel has an alibi. She's not the killer. I don't know if she's told them yet, but I can back her up. Of course, that'll also involve coming clean about the fact that I followed her into the woods, but there's a dozen innocent reasons I might have been there, and I can't let her stay in jail when she's the one person who *didn't* do it."

Whether she was guilty or not, Steve the Gargoyle knew hardly anything about the reality of the situation and didn't care to learn more. He could have vital evidence staring him in the face and he probably wouldn't know it. Just look at Mr Bayer. If Steve couldn't think to fly over the fence of someone who kept important evidence in his garden right next to the crime scene, I'd bet my non-existent wand that he'd utterly missed obvious evidence this time around as well.

"Ah," said Alissa. "Yeah, that's a dilemma, but you know what Steve's like. Ask Nathan to back you up?"

"He already got me out of jail once."

"Ooh. See, told you it's meant to be."

I swatted half-heartedly at her. "Oi, focus. We have a situation to deal with. Can Madame Grey help?"

"I'll give her a call, but I doubt she'd support your plan."

"I know. But I need to tell the police that the mice were once people. It's fairly pertinent information. It's not like it proves *I* did anything."

"No, you're right. I'll come with you and wait outside, then. He knows Madame Grey is my grandmother, and to be honest, she probably scared him when she demanded he let you go. She does that."

"Good." There was possibly nothing I wanted to do *less* than walk right into Steve's office, but this needed to be dealt with. The police station might be guarded by terrifying gargoyles, but it definitely didn't have a hundred activated wands waiting to scare off intruders. At least I could count on that much.

———

Once I had reassurance that Alissa had my back, I swallowed my pride and walked to Steve's office. The police station, which stood adjacent to the jail, was more modern than the dungeon-style place I'd been stuck in overnight, though it was still packed with huge muscle-bound gargoyles.

"Guilty conscience?" said Steve, as I entered.

"No, I have evidence to deliver."

He grunted and beckoned me into an office to the side. "Your funeral." Just the sort of thing you wanted to hear in the home of the local law enforcement.

He planted himself in a desk chair that made him look like an adult sitting at a children's picnic table, and looked me over. "You seem more substantial than before."

"Yes, the potion wore off. I heard you arrested Annabel, the seer's granddaughter."

"Who told you?"

"Madame Grey," I answered, knowing he wouldn't retaliate against that name. He might run the show here, but the witches still owned the town.

The gargoyle glowered at me. "Yes, we arrested the girl. She's our key suspect at the moment."

"Uh—why?"

"She rang him the morning he died, according to her call history."

"That doesn't prove she murdered him," I countered. "I actually saw her in the forest at the time when he died."

"You're not a reliable witness, being a suspect yourself," he said.

"You mean, former suspect," I said, gripping the sides of the chair. "Have you managed to search his shop yet?"

He scowled. "No."

"And did you, er, find any mice near the crime scene?"

He rose to his feet. "Did you come here to waste my time?"

"No, of course not." I should have guessed he wouldn't listen. "May I speak with the prisoner?"

"No," he said, "you may *not* talk to the prisoner."

I grimaced. So much for Plan A. "My witch power allows me to sense if someone's lying," I told him. "So—"

"So that's why you fancy yourself a detective?" He snorted. "Anyone can sense deceit if they spend long enough around criminals."

Oh, no. I'd thought playing my best card might actually work. Now I was out of options and out of luck.

I left before he decided to lock me up again, and found Alissa waiting with her hands in her pockets. "Any luck?"

"None whatsoever. He refused to let me get a word in edgeways, so I told him about my witch power. Even *that* didn't work. I need a miracle to get through his rock-hard skull." Never mind an invisibility potion. "Is there a potion for…?" I trailed off. "Lucky latte."

"Don't get any ideas," she said. "They work, but you know the side effects."

Lucky lattes. Unlike potions, they could be bought from any coffee shop in town. I didn't need to brew up a potion to get a brief stroke of luck. And to be honest, I'd take five *minutes* of decent luck at the moment. That was all I needed to solve the case. I should have taken one of those from the start.

"I know, I'll have god-awful luck for the next week and probably fail the exam," I said, "but to be honest, the last few days have felt like I've been suffering the backlash of a bad luck charm, anyway. There's nothing more I can do. If nothing else, it might help me find those mice."

"Hmm," she said. "A lucky latte is less harmful than accidental transparency. But it probably won't get you through to Steve. And the other problem with those lattes is that everyone will remember what you did after the spell wears off, so if you break the law, the consequences will reach you as soon as your luck runs out."

That sounded ominous. "What, like going back to the crime scene? Wouldn't it be lucky if nobody sees me?"

"Yes, but you don't get to choose how your streak of good luck manifests. And the police are watching the scene."

My shoulders slumped. "The mice are still in there. I just need to get hold of one of them. That's all."

"It's not a bad shout," she said. "But you don't know what those mice look like, so if you pick the wrong one and your luck runs out before the potion is complete, you'll have a field mouse bleating in your ear for the next day."

I groaned. "Can't it ever be simple?"

"Nope," she said. "Of all the people you suspected, who hasn't been jailed?"

"Ava, for a start," I said. "Her granddaughter's in jail… not sure about that elf she was meeting with. I think Ava is my best bet. I already have a good enough reason to enter the hospital."

I just needed to make the right call this time. I'd already messed that up thoroughly with the transparency. This time I might not be so lucky, latte or not.

She shook her head. "Are you really sure? You might be throwing away your chance, if you get caught."

"I've already pretty much lost my shot at getting a wand. And these people are facing a lifetime in jail—or stuck as rodents—if I don't help them out."

"If you're sure," Alissa said.

"I am."

No transparency this time. Just me, my wits, and as much luck as I could conjure.

13

Alissa told me that the best place to procure a lucky latte was Charms & Caffeine, the most popular coffee shop on the high street. It also happened to be where Lizzie's sister worked.

I made my way over to the counter. It was easy to recognise Layla, who had the same warm brown skin and wide smile as her sister. Her hair was braided into a topknot. "Hey," I said to her. "We haven't met, but I'm Blair. I work with your sister."

She beamed. "You're the newbie, right? What can I get you?"

"I'd like to try a lucky latte."

Her brows shot up. "We only do those on special occasions. Anyway—not that it's any of my business, but aren't you supposed to be taking an exam soon? It's illegal to take luck potions beforehand."

Maybe I needed a shot of luck just to get my hands on some. "Not until tomorrow," I said. "Just for a few hours. It's pretty urgent. I don't know if your sister told you, but Mr

Falconer was my client. And he died and left a real mess behind. I need some serious luck to sort it out."

"I shouldn't," she said. "But since you know Lizzie, and I heard what you did for Mr Bayer, this one's on the house."

"Thanks so much."

Once she'd handed me my lucky latte, I drank it down. It tasted of soap, and I nearly spat it out again. "I can tell why people don't make a habit of drinking this stuff."

She grinned. "Sorry. I should have warned you."

Alissa laughed. "I've never taken one," she said, in answer to my accusing stare.

"Oh," I said. Then: "*Oh.*"

A heady sensation rippled through my body like stepping off a rollercoaster, giving me a sense of weightlessness even on the ground. Like I'd accidentally turned on the highest setting on my levitating boots—or had my wings out. Hey, that was a great idea.

Alissa grabbed my arm, and I became aware that I'd raised both arms at right angles like a child impersonating a super-hero. "Focus, Blair. You had a plan. Right?"

I nodded, but my head was in the clouds. I *wanted* to fly. To remove my glamour. But without the waterfall, I couldn't, and—*Mr Falconer. The mice. Annabel.*

I skipped out of the coffee shop, oblivious to any stares, and danced into the shop next door, a flower shop. Less than a minute later and I bounded away with a bouquet of flowers that flashed like traffic lights.

"What's that for?" Alissa asked. "Blair, I don't think you're thinking clearly."

"It's a gift. For Ava." And I was off again, down the road. I managed to slow down when I entered the hospital, and casually walked to the ward.

"Hey," I said to the nearest nurse. "I came to give these to

Ava, to tell her how sorry I am about her granddaughter's arrest."

If my luck had been at its usual levels, she'd have taken them and told me to get lost, but she merely nodded, her expression slightly dazed. Another side effect? Whatever it was, I wasn't complaining.

Ava appeared a moment later, as dishevelled as ever, but her eyes gleamed with amusement. "She's elf-struck," said Ava, jerking her head in the direction of the nurse. "The elf got her when she wasn't looking."

"Wait, there's an elf here?"

"Yes, in the ward next door."

Alissa prodded me in the arm, whispering, "We some-times have elves in here. Focus."

"I thought elves only had weather magic?"

Ava cackled. "For the most part, but when they're really annoyed, they can also befuddle the senses. They sometimes do it to the witches who wander too close to their territory in the forest."

Territory... "Like the witches? The wand-makers?"

"Crooks," she muttered.

"Who, Mr Falconer?" I dropped my voice. "Or the others? Have you heard of the Wormwood Coven?"

She eyed me with an appraising look. "You know of them?"

"I heard they were... they're the ones who pay for the wand supplies. For Mr Falconer. But you made one, too. Do you remember why you ended up coming in here?"

Luck couldn't jolt someone's memory, but she was lucid sometimes. I crossed my fingers that this was one of those moments.

"An accident," she said, dropping her voice dramatically. *Truth.*

"Your granddaughter thought Mr Falconer was responsible," I said.

"Oh, not at all," she said. "She was angry with him at the time, because he fired her with no warning."

I gaped at her, all my other questions forgotten. Ava's granddaughter had been Mr Falconer's apprentice.

How had she gone through my questioning and not let that slip?

"Why… why him? Why does it have to be him?"

She cackled again. "They have him by the throat. They might not remember the wand-making craft, but they'll see to it that he makes wands until he dies."

"He did die," I whispered. "Is the coven—are the original wand-makers alive? Did they forget on purpose, or…?"

Alissa trod on my foot, hard. "Blair. The nurse is coming. We have to go."

"Okay." I took a step backwards. I'd learned what I needed to—*I think.*

But Annabel had managed to get around my lie-sensing ability. She'd been aware of it the whole time and had deliberately skirted around the truth to stop me from guessing. Why?

———

When a nurse accosted Alissa on the way out of the hospital, I sneaked out and went on the hunt for Annabel. The idea that Steve might refuse me entry to the jail crossed my mind, but despite the shock of Ava's revelation, the humming sensation of the lucky latte buzzed in my veins like a lingering caffeine high.

Part of me was unsurprised to run into the woman herself walking down the road from the jail. "Annabel?"

"Blair," she said, not sounding thrilled. "What are you doing here? I heard you were arrested, too."

"They let me out. They did the same to you?"

She nodded. "Not enough evidence. Apparently the spell that killed him was too advanced for me to have cast it. It—was one of his own wands."

"Seriously?" I stared at her. "That—wow. Did they tell you anything else?"

"I wasn't supposed to hear that part. Were you going back there now?"

"To speak to you," I said. "You were Mr Falconer's apprentice."

Her eyes narrowed, and I braced myself—to run, or call for help.

"I just want the truth. You were really his apprentice?"

Her shoulders slumped. "Yes, I was. Two years ago. My grandmother wasn't happy about it. She thought I could do better."

I couldn't say I was surprised. "Because of her own wand-making business?"

"No, that came later. I quit my apprenticeship, because I was seeing someone."

"An elf." I doubted the wand-maker would have been happy that his apprentice was messing around with one of his enemies, not to mention the elves themselves were morally opposed to wand-making.

Her eyes widened. "How did you guess?"

"Never mind." I pleaded with the luck potion to hold. "So you left?"

"I didn't want him finding out, so I quit. But he wasn't too happy. He thought my grandmother was responsible. They traded angry letters for a bit, apparently."

I kept nodding, certain that this time was going to bring me to the answer. Two old people trading cantankerous spells was convincing enough, and her words rang with sincerity—but still, neither she nor her grandmother struck me as a potential murderer, any more than they had before. Especially now I knew the real reason for her lies.

"Anyway, she confronted him, at our house. When he pulled his wand out, she hexed him and turned his hair purple. They haven't spoken since."

I nearly laughed. "That's all she did?"

"Yes." She exhaled in a sigh. "And then she set up her own business… and then her accident happened, and that was the end of it."

"Do you… think he might have been involved?" I asked hesitantly.

Her mouth thinned. "She wasn't—I told you she wasn't in her right mind, before that. She was no threat to him."

"But you *were* his apprentice. And I heard he doesn't like his secrets getting out."

Annabel shook her head. "We never reached most of the secrets. I was just chopping wood into sticks most of the time. He let me use my own wand occasionally, but he said I had to learn discipline."

"He never sent you gathering wandwood?"

"He probably would have if I'd stayed long enough. But I still don't know how he actually imbues the wands with life, or whatever it is that makes them tick. The wands just sit there most of the time. I know there are a few secret spells he uses on them, complicated ones. I was due to learn it all eventually, but I don't think he was committed to training an apprentice. He didn't even do much wand-making. Spent most of his time wandering around the forest or just in his office. Whatever he was working on, he didn't want me involved."

Weird. "So did you or Ava put a curse on him? I have to

ask, because the people who were affected still aren't turning back even though he's dead."

She shook her head. "I didn't. Neither did Ava, to my knowledge."

"How long were you his apprentice for?" I asked.

"Just over a week."

Not long enough for the curse to come into effect. Was there some issue with this secret knowledge that caused it, or was someone determined that nobody else learn the secrets of wand-making? If so—who exactly were they? Did Ava's ramblings hold some truth—and if so, how had nobody else guessed?

"Okay," I said. "He wasn't bothered about teaching you, then. Did he seem to be... really obsessive over his job? Is that why he wouldn't talk to you?"

She frowned. "No. I got the impression he didn't *like* the position, but he refused to speak about himself at all."

"Wait, he didn't like it? Wand-making?" I'd assumed that he was grumpy because he cared only for wand-making. So why did he carry on doing it?

When I asked, she just shrugged. "No clue. If anything, I'd say the evidence is in his shop, so maybe the police have already found it."

They haven't. They never managed to get in.

I doubted he'd left diaries of his deepest life confessions lying around, and in any case, my newfound luck probably wouldn't extend to getting past whatever spells he'd left on the wands guarding the doors to his shop. I'd eliminated the most likely suspects, and my luck was running out right before an exam that might affect my entire future as a witch.

No pressure, Blair.

14

Back to square one. I'd been so certain Annabel had been behind the curse at the very least, and now she'd gone, I had no idea what to do with myself. My phone buzzed with a text from Alissa. The hospital had roped her into doing an extra shift, since she was there. She wasn't kidding about the lucky lattes not having much consideration for other people's luck. Worse, the light, tingling feeling in my body was beginning to fade, and even if I flew, I might not reach Mr Falconer's shop before it ran out.

I turned back to the jail, indecision tearing at me—and Nathan walked out of the doors.

If ever there was a *bad* time to run into him, it was now.

"Blair?" he said, in puzzlement. "What are you doing here?"

"I ran into Annabel," I improvised. "Didn't know they let her out."

"Oh, she's been found innocent," he said. "Is there any reason you're back here?"

"I—Mr Falconer's apprentices. They're still missing."

"Well, they're not here," he said. "I don't think you should be wandering around here, either, considering."

He was right. What had I been thinking? Answer: I hadn't, thanks to that latte. "What are you doing? Did they have you search the crime scene?"

"They did," he said. "Why?"

"They said one of his own wands was responsible for his death," I said.

He raised an eyebrow. "Who said that?"

"Annabel did. It… to be honest, it doesn't sound like the gargoyles have the expertise here." I cast a look over my shoulder, wondering if I could inject my last piece of luck into convincing him to explore the crime scene with me.

"They'll have to call in an expert, I imagine," said Nathan. "If you want to talk about this, it's probably not the best place. Tell you what… want to come to the Troll's Tavern again? This time, hopefully your cat will behave."

My heart skipped a beat. He was asking me out. Maybe… maybe my luck wasn't out after all, but it had transferred over from the murder case. I mean, if Mr Falconer's wand had killed him, Annabel was innocent, and so was Ava, and I no longer needed to be involved.

If only I could banish the sliver of doubt in my mind… and a few cocktails would take care of that. Though I knew my past experience with alcohol was questionable even when I wasn't suffering the backlash of an unsuccessful lucky latte.

"I can," I said. "I used a lucky latte, but didn't get anything useful out of anyone. And now it's backfiring, so fair warning. You might want to stand a little further away in case a roof beam falls on my head or something."

"I'll risk it. Come and tell me all about it," he said.

Are you sure? I swallowed down the words and did my best to put what Annabel had said out of mind. I finally had a shot with Nathan. That was worth putting my wild theories on hold for.

Nathan walked closer to me than usual as we made for the Troll's Tavern. Or maybe my senses were heightened due to the excitement of the week, the aftermath of the spell, and my ongoing paranoia that I'd forgotten something really, really important.

When we reached the pub, however, my heart sank. At a table near the doors sat a person I'd hoped not to see again, or at least for a few years. Blythe.

Yeah, my luck was backfiring, all right.

As we passed by, she looked in my direction. As a witch with mind-reading abilities, she'd have been able to pick up on my thoughts the instant I entered the pub. I ignored her and walked with Nathan to the same table we'd picked out last time, hoping he hadn't spotted her. She'd tried to drive a wedge between the two of us before and almost succeeded, but with her wand bound, the worst she could do was insert herself into our date and make a nuisance of herself.

After he went to speak to the bartender, she sidled over to my table. There was little point in pretending I hadn't seen her, and Blythe's wand was permanently fixed so she couldn't cast any dangerous spells, including the hexes she'd once used on me. "Blythe," I said nonchalantly. "To what do I owe the pleasure?"

"So you're here with Nathan? Have you told him yet?"

"Told him what?" I said. "Look, if you don't mind, I've had a highly stressful week, and I'm intending to get raging drunk and forget all about it."

She sniffed. "Like him?"

I followed her gaze to a table nearby, where a young man sat surrounded by empty glasses. Leopold. I never did check up on how he'd coped after being fired.

I got to my feet, sidestepped Blythe and made my way

over to him, leaving her blinking after me, as though she was hardly able to believe I had the nerve to pretend she didn't exist.

"Are you okay?" I asked.

Leopold jumped. "Yes."

"You're drinking your body weight in witch cocktails," I pointed out. "Your apprenticeship with Mr Falconer didn't go well, right?"

He took another shot. "You might say that."

"Was he mean to you? I suppose I don't have to ask."

"He's mean to everyone," said Leopold. "He refused to teach me anything, just ordered me to sit there chopping wood all day."

That fit with what I'd heard from Annabel, too. "You were only there for a couple of days, right? What did he teach you in that time? He must have explained where the wood came from."

"Sure, the forest. He has the elves take it and sell it to him."

"He… has the elves do it? I thought they hated him."

"I don't know about the bloody elves, do I? I just did what he said and got yelled at for it. I never even got paid."

"You didn't? I guess you didn't stay long enough."

He shrugged. "He basically said he wouldn't be able to pay me the minimum salary, and that I should only stay if I loved the work. I said I didn't, and he kicked me out. But he never planned to pay me anyway. He was broke."

My mouth fell open. "What? Seriously? How's that possible?"

He picked up one of the few non-empty glasses and drank what was left in it. "Don't ask me."

I wanted to ask *someone*. He had all those wands, which were worth a small fortune. Unless the academy's discounts were steeper than I'd thought. *That coven... they provide the funding.*

"Okay, but it doesn't matter now he's dead, does it?" I said. "I don't suppose you know who might have done it?"

"No." He got to his feet and sloped off to the bar.

Well, that changed things. What had Mr Falconer been doing with the money from the wands? Was he hoarding the profits for some other means? Or did he owe someone money? Just when I thought I was closer to answers, they slipped through my grip again.

"Blair?" said Nathan, walking back over from the bar.

"Sorry," I said, joining him back at the table, which was thankfully Blythe-free. "Leopold was Mr Falconer's last apprentice. I know the police said he didn't see anything, but I just wanted to check. It's bizarre, but Falconer was flat broke, apparently. I don't suppose you have any idea what he might have been doing with the profits from the wands?"

He shook his head, taking his seat. "No, I can't say I spoke with the man. I thought you were done with the case."

I sat opposite him. "Not until I get those mice turned into people again. This new information—it sounds like he was barely making a profit from the wands. That doesn't really fit with what I know about him."

And where did the elves fit, if he'd been trading with them all along?

"You don't have to think about all this," he insisted. "Like I said—it's out of your hands. You should relax."

"I'm a little on edge, thanks to that luck potion. If one of us gets mauled by a unicorn, that's why."

He smiled. "The side effects are a pain, but not so much that anything will go tragically wrong. There's a reason the more powerful strands of luck potion were banned. And luck spells."

"Banned?" I echoed. "So there are banned potions as well as spells? How do they keep track of that type of thing?"

He picked up his beer glass and took a drink. "Not well enough. I'm pretty sure they put boundaries around the wands themselves, at least at first."

Boundaries. "How does that work?"

"I'm not a wizard," he said. "You'll have to ask Madame Grey, or one of the academy staff, if you want to know in more detail. But as far as I know, the wands are doctored with a spell that causes them to shut down when someone attempts an illegal spell."

"I didn't know you could put a spell *on* a wand," I admitted. Wait—Madame Grey had mentioned something along those lines. About the rules being changed since she'd got her own wand.

Wait a minute.

No way. I was jumping to conclusions. I still hadn't gathered all the evidence… but there were an awful lot of wands in that shop. Since the wands were identical and their owner wasn't particularly attentive…

"Of course you can," he said.

I sat up rigidly. "Oh, no. I think I know what happened."

"What?" he asked.

"The curse is on one of the *wands,*" I said. "If the curse is on an object, it doesn't matter that he's dead, because it'll stay in effect, I guess as long as the wand is around. He probably doesn't even check his own wands, because they all look identical. That means it's still there. If we find it, we can turn the mice back into humans."

He shook his head. "I highly doubt he wouldn't have noticed. It's been a year."

"Yes, but he doesn't check the shelves. Leopold told me he never did much wand-making at all."

"Are you sure?"

"It adds up. And if the wands get transferred to the academy, someone innocent might get hurt. I don't know if he was the target and just protected himself too well, but it's not worth the risk. What if it's true and one of the wands killed him? The same one?"

There was a long pause. Then Nathan nodded. "You're right. Let's see if we can get into that shop."

15

The sky had properly darkened by now, and the moonlight threw the dark buildings into sharp relief. My heart drummed in anticipation. I knew my theory was right, though the pieces hadn't completely fallen into place yet. With Nathan at my side, I felt much safer, even if I'd have to face the backlash if this went wrong. And odds were, something probably would go wrong. After all, I'd left my good luck streak behind with the latte.

"If Steve couldn't get in, we might not be able to, either," Nathan said. "The wands still need to be moved to another location. It's a problem when someone like him dies, because it takes special attention to deal with magic-related security. And the police don't have that expertise… don't tell Steve I said that."

I grinned despite myself. "Does he want a repeat of Mr Bayer's garden and the killer plants? He should have had someone take care of the issue by now. I can't figure out where those mice disappeared to, either. That was supposed to be my plan—find one of them and use a spell so I'd be able to understand their speech."

"Hmm." He frowned, looking at the window as we drew to a halt outside Mr Falconer's shop. "There's a light on in there."

So there was. Maybe I should have waited for the aftereffects of the not-so-lucky backlash to wear off before doing anything risky. But we were already here.

"Is it locked?" I asked.

"It shouldn't be." He pushed the door. It didn't give. "Maybe the police came back."

I shoved it, stupidly, even though I knew perfectly well he was much stronger than I was. But after one shove from both of us, the door swung inwards.

I stared into the shop's dark, cold interior, which looked the same as usual, down to the mouse cage on the desk. Faint squeaking came from within. *Aha.*

I reached for the cage, and the door slammed behind me. "Hey!" I grabbed the door, alarm blaring through me, but it didn't budge. Footsteps sounded in the gloom. Dread gripped my chest. "Who's there?"

I didn't need to ask. Mr Falconer stood there, very much alive. Not transparent, but solid, and terrifying.

I raised my hands. "I know who did it," I said. "But— you're alive. You faked your death. Why?"

"So they'd leave me alone," he growled. "Including the likes of you."

"You're the one who kept calling me." I raised my voice over the pounding in my chest. "What are you doing here? You should know the police are still investigating." With every word, I backed up closer to the door, but it was still wedged shut. By magic.

"The police won't bother me," he said. "It's time you gave me the answers, Blair."

"You locked me in," I said. "Are you going to kill me, too?"

"I shouldn't need to, as long as you give me the answers I want."

He was actually deranged.

"You nearly got me locked up for murder," I said. "And the apprentices—you're hiding them here, aren't you?"

"I can't have them wandering around outside," he said.

"Why, because someone might catch one of them and manage to pry your secrets out of them?"

"As a matter of fact, yes," he said. "I don't want them talking."

"About how you were a terrible mentor?" I asked. "They don't need to. Annabel told me, and she's not happy to be blamed for your murder, either."

"I should have known that one would gossip." He took a step closer to me, a wand in his hand. "Tell me where the curse is."

So he really didn't know.

"It's on one of the wands," I said. "I don't know which, or how it got here…" But maybe I did.

"You're being ridiculous. Nobody could have messed with one of my wands. I'd know."

"Apparently you didn't." He spoke the truth—my lie-sensing ability picked up on that, if nothing else—but maybe it was what he believed to be the truth, not reality.

"Has a wand ever been returned here before, from outside?" I asked him. "What happens when its owner dies? Or it's confiscated?"

I had to hand it to Ava. I also didn't think she'd meant to hit his apprentices, but who knew what was going through her head?

His eyes narrowed. "Yes. Confiscated wands are returned here."

"Ava," I said. "She left a last surprise for you." A clever one, too. "But that's not all there is," I said. "You're being blackmailed, aren't you? By the surviving members of the Worm-wood Coven, the ones who made themselves forget the craft of wand-making."

His jaw clenched. I'd got it right.

"Those treacherous old witches," he growled. "They prob-ably put her up to it to begin with."

"You mean the ones you intimidated into erasing their own memories?"

"I intimidated *them?*" he snapped. "No. I only wanted to teach them a little humility, but they had the last laugh. Nobody carries a grudge like a witch."

"You wiped their memories, so they cursed you to make wands for the rest of your life and hand over the profits to them? Seems fair to me. But it's *not* fair to leave your appren-tices like that." I took a cautious step towards the cage.

"I can't let you help them," he said. "The witches and I have an understanding, but they will take everything I have if the truth comes out. Lift the curse and I'll let you leave with the mice."

"I don't know how to lift the curse. You'll have to find the wand yourself." My gaze went to the mice, then to the fancy wand in the window display.

"That thing." He swore under his breath. "I should have known."

Crossing the shop floor, he picked it up in his hand. "This one won't obey me."

Because it was an older branch of wand, from before his own method had been standardised.

"The elves," I said, seeing he had no apparent inclination to open the door and let me out. "Friends or foes?"

"Depends on the day of the week."

Which explained nothing. "They hated you... or worked with you. Or is it the witches they hate?"

"We have that in common," he growled. "The Wormwood

Coven are crooks. I suppose they became worried when I began to pass on the trade secrets to others."

"But you've had other apprentices, before these ones," I said. "Right?"

"Aside from that girl? No." He shook the wand, turning it over in his hand.

"The mice aren't turning back," I said. "Look, you're going to have to hand over that wand to a curse expert to undo it. Or the caster."

"I don't think so." An ugly expression crossed his face. "Besides, I can't have those apprentices blabbing."

I took a step backwards, ready to bolt for the door, even knowing it was locked against me. "So why hire me to break the curse in the first place?"

"Why else? I needed to know who my enemy was, and if I had anything to fear from them. Now I know." He took a step towards me. "You'll be staying here for a little while. A long while. At least you won't be alone."

He raised the wand.

"I wouldn't," I warned him. "Nathan's outside. Either of us could bring the police to you in a second."

"The police know nothing about this place."

Several wands sparked, and something flashed outside the doors—right where Nathan had been waiting. My heart lurched. I couldn't see if he'd been hit or if he'd managed to get out of the way.

I backed up towards the shelves. I might not have a wand of my own, but I was a walking force of destruction and the shelves were old and wobbly. It wouldn't take too much effort to knock them over.

He raised the wand. I kicked out, and the nearest set of shelves crashed down. An explosion of light went off to my left, but missed. I leapt behind the collapsed shelf and kicked wildly at the next one, causing a domino effect of sparks and crashing lights. Mr Falconer swore, showers of sparks exploding over his head. I threw myself out of the way, and landed on my back as wands crashed to the ground.

Grimacing, I groped around for something—anything to defend myself with. My fingers closed around a wand handle and an odd tingling sensation ran straight from my fingertips. I picked it up, and sparks shot from the end.

Frantic squeaking erupted somewhere close by. I got to my feet, rubbing the back of my head. The dust cleared, revealing Mr Falconer, surrounded by mice. One of them held his wand out of reach in its paws.

He roared and grabbed for it, and I raised my own wand in defence.

A rush of heat enveloped my hand, and a shimmering barrier appeared in front of me.

"DO NOT DEFEND HER," he screamed. It took me a moment to realise he'd yelled at the wand, not the mice.

Of course. The wand in my hand was still programmed to defend the place against harm, except now it'd chosen me, I was included in the spell. It would never let him harm me.

He climbed to his feet. "YOU DARE—"

A blast went off from the window display where the wand had fallen, and he crumpled to the floor, shrinking in on himself. A moment later, nothing remained but another, grey-furred mouse.

There was a long pause, where the dust settled. The other mice edged away as though reluctant to go within a metre of him even as a rodent.

"Nice." I walked over, picking him up by the tail. "Where's that cage?"

One of the other former apprentices squeaked at me, indicating the place the cage had fallen to the floor. I returned it to the desk and dropped him into it.

"I was thinking jail would work for him," I said. "But maybe he should stay in there for a while instead."

More squeaking drew my attention to the door. One of the mice nudged it open, and Nathan ran in—accompanied by two gargoyles.

"Get this to the coven,' I said, holding up Ava's silver wand. "It was Ava's old wand, and it had a curse on it before it was confiscated. I'm not sure if she remembers—or for all I know, he erased her memories himself. I'm sure he's capable of it."

"Where is he?" asked Nathan, looking from the wand in my hand to the collapsed shelves and scattered boxes with a slightly stunned expression on his face.

I indicated the mouse cage. "That's him. We can't reverse the curse without knowing who cast it, so... I guess he's going to have to stay like that for a bit."

16

"My wand!" Ava shrieked in delight, lunging to take it from me and cradling it in her hands.

To my immense surprise, the gargoyles had agreed to come and talk to her at the hospital. Probably because they hadn't understood a word of my explanation and they thought the old seer might be able to offer more of a clue. When I'd told them the wand was cursed, they kept their distance and let me carry it. Pity it only worked on apprentices, because I thought Steve deserved to have a shot at being a mouse. Just long enough for my cat to chase him around for a bit.

I was pleased to know that while the gargoyles didn't have any qualms about locking me up, doing the same to hospitalised pensioners was a step too far. If she was the caster, the curse would undo at her command.

"Stop crowding her," snapped Annabel, who'd also been called in. "The wand is hers."

Ava turned the silver wand over in her hand, and I lifted the cage of mice onto my lap. "Did you cast this spell?" I asked her.

She peered into the cage. "Who are they?"

"Mr Falconer's apprentices," I said. "They got hit by a curse someone put on your wand. I know it's possible for someone else to curse a wand if it doesn't belong to anyone, but in this case… you know, it's not your fault the curse hit the wrong target."

She blinked. "Curse?"

My inner lie detector didn't go off, but I nodded. "Yep. Just point the wand at them, and—"

There was a flash of light, and several people—notably the gargoyles—ducked for cover.

And suddenly there were a lot more people in the room.

Ava gave a slight laugh. "That was meant to hit the person who confiscated it from me. Spoilsports." She glared at the nearest nurse.

My mouth dropped open. "That's who you tried to hit? Not Mr Falconer?"

"I never said I had an accurate aim."

I nearly laughed, imagining how Mr Falconer would react. The whole time, he'd thought someone was plotting against him, but he hadn't even been the intended target. He'd have a while as a rodent to think on his own crimes, at least.

The nearest gargoyle looked at his phone. "Madame Grey wishes to meet with us to discuss the future of the wand-making trade." He looked around as though hoping someone else would take over.

"Ask Mr Falconer," I said. "That wand can turn him human again, but he's definitely committed crimes against the Wormwood Coven. He erased all their memories of the craft, so they retaliated by making him the only wand-maker."

Everyone stared at me. Then one of the apprentices said, "She's right. I heard him ranting at them."

"I saw him yelling at the elves in the wood. They're in on it, too."

"He said they were extorting him."

"So he was blackmailed, essentially," I explained. "But he started it by erasing the memories of the coven who used to practise wand-work. I don't know where they live, but Madame Grey will."

"We will convene with her, then," said the gargoyle. "And take this wand to the jail so that the wand-maker may take his trial as a man, not a mouse."

Oh well. You can't have it all.

———

"How do you think it went?" asked Alissa, when she met me outside the door of the examination room.

I shook my head. "No clue. I hope it went better than I think, but I'm a little short on luck at the moment."

"I was waiting for something to explode again," she admitted.

"So little faith. Even I can't blow up a test paper. Or turn it transparent."

"Ha. Whether you pass or not, you're free to come with me to buy some accessories for that new wand now, right?"

I grinned. Whether I passed the test or not, I felt pretty pleased with myself. "Sounds good to me."

I had a wand. And my first order of business was to improve its generic design with something more 'me'.

———

I looked at the rows of accessories in the shop. Brightly coloured ribbons weren't my thing, and anything that was likely to become detached or get caught on my hand when I was casting a spell was an accident waiting to happen.

My gaze skimmed the shelves, then landed on a pair of wings. "Hmm."

"Do it," said Alissa. "They're perfect."

I clipped the wings onto the end of the wand, twirling it in my fingertips and nearly dropping it. "I draw the line at glitter. I don't want to have to clean it out of the carpet every time I cast a spell."

"You could just vanish it."

I smiled. "You really want that to be the first spell I try, after the transparency fiasco? I might accidentally on purpose make Blythe disappear…"

"Where'd she fit into all this, anyway?" asked Alissa.

"She doesn't. She's still disgraced, but I guess they let her off early for good behaviour. Long enough for her to attempt to sabotage my date with Nathan… if I hadn't sabotaged it myself by going after Mr Falconer."

"Pretty sure he'll forgive you for that."

I looked at the wings. A simple clue, but one that could upend the new life I'd only just begun to build here. Those weird dreams I'd been having lately… they were a sign that I still hadn't figured out my heritage. My family's past. I wanted to talk to Ava again, one way or another. If Annabel wasn't too mad at me. But everyone accused was freed, the mice were people again, and I had a wand. Life was good.

Helen waited for me outside. "Hey, Blair."

"Hey," I said, surprised to see her.

"I just wanted to say I'm glad you solved that case," she said. "I—I'm partly related to the original leaders of the Wormwood Coven, and I thought there was something not quite right about the way the wand-making business ended up. But I didn't know they had Mr Falconer under a spell."

"Wait, they won't be punished for this, right?" I asked.

"That's up to Madame Grey," she said, "who sent me to tell you that you passed the exam."

My jaw dropped. "I did?"

"Yes." Her sunny smile snapped back into place.

I smiled back. "Thanks for letting me know."

"Are you sure you don't want to come and join us at the fete later today? We'll have ice cream."

"You know, I might just do that. Let me get back to you." I turned to Alissa. "I guess my luck wasn't as deficient as I thought."

"That, or you retained some of Rita's lectures," Alissa said. "She's a good teacher. Though fair warning, you probably won't be able to get away with that in the practical tests. Wands backfire when you aren't paying attention. And potions. I feel like she'll want to see your invisibility potion-making skills."

"I should have known she'd get me back for that."

When we got back to the flat, I found Sky stretched out on the sofa, waiting for a stroke. I petted him. "You were trying to warn me, weren't you?"

"Miaow."

"Thanks," I said to Sky. "I think. I still won't rule out using that speaking spell on you next time you bring something questionable into the flat. I don't need mice in my room, thanks."

"Miaow."

I took that to mean "no more mice". Or possibly "feed me."

"Hey, he didn't destroy the bubble wrap this time," said Alissa. "As far as I'm concerned, that means he's officially supporting your relationship with Nathan."

"We've had one and a half dates. And I'm not sure how to explain this." I waved the wand, and the wall turned purple. "What? Isn't the safety setting on?"

Alissa laughed. "I think Mr Falconer used to do that manually. They're sold without the setting on so they can pick out their owner easily."

She waved her own wand and the wall turned back to its former colour.

"You're going to be cleaning up after me a lot, I think," I said, putting the wand carefully in its case and laying it on the table next to the sofa.

"I'll live. It'll be worth it to have two wands to help around the house."

I stroked Sky. "Don't get ahead of yourself. I'm not the fastest learner."

I had another stack of books to read, more tests coming around the corner, and I couldn't be happier about it. Oh, and no mice in my underwear drawer was always a bonus.

"I'm glad we're free from rodents," I said. "Guess he was just helping the apprentices, not being a mighty hunter."

"Oh, some of them were real," Alissa said. "Roald ate them."

I pulled a face. "Definitely none of the candidates?"

"Nope. They're happily human again."

"And so am I. Sort of."

The doorbell rang. Alissa looked at me. "Hmm. Expecting anyone?"

"No... maybe." I wasn't, but... hey, maybe the lucky latte hadn't worn off after all.

I opened the door. A letter lay on the doorstep, an envelope with curling writing on it. Addressed to me.

To Blair,

I would very much like to meet you.

Please come to the waterfall at the solstice.

Sincerely,

Your family.

ABOUT THE AUTHOR

Elle Adams lives in the middle of England, where she spends most of her time reading an ever-growing mountain of books, planning her next adventure, or writing. Elle's books are humorous mysteries with a paranormal twist, packed with magical mayhem.

She also writes urban and contemporary fantasy novels as Emma L. Adams.

Find Elle on Facebook at https://www.facebook.com/pg/ElleAdamsAuthor/